# THE
# STRANGER'S
## BED

# THE
# STRANGER'S
## BED

OLIVER SANDS

deGrevilo Publishing

Cataloguing in Publication details are available from the National Library of Australia www.trove.nla.gov.au

Creator: Sands, Oliver
Title: The Stranger's Bed / Oliver Sands

ISBN: 978-0-6487448-3-2 (paperback)
ISBN: 978-0-6487448-2-5 (e-book)

Set in Times New Roman 12 pt

Disclaimer: This is a work of fiction. The characters contained within its pages are wholly imaginary. Any resemblance to actual persons, living or dead, or events, is entirely coincidental. The places depicted have been re-imagined to suit the convenience of the story. The opinions expressed are those of the characters and should not be confused with the author's own.

For more information on the author and his books visit
www.OliverSandsAuthor.com

# October

# ONE

ANNA SHIFTS IN THE PASSENGER SEAT and tugs the rough edge of the frayed seat belt away from her neck. Her clapped-out Fiesta whines in complaint as Dan shifts down into third gear beside her. He's not accustomed to driving a manual on these rural Irish roads and now he curses to himself as the front wheel clips another pothole. Anna nibbles at a piece of loose skin by her thumbnail, then turns to check the backseat.

'Dan?'

'Hmm?'

'Did you put my gym bag in the boot?' She looks at his side profile, sees the frown bloom on his tanned forehead. But even as she awaits his answer, Anna can picture the sports bag, still sitting by the foot of the stairs where she set it down for a moment, Dan droning on about getting a head start on the Friday afternoon Dublin traffic.

'No, love. I didn't touch it.'

She turns around in her seat, closes her eyes and tilts her head back against the rigid headrest. 'Damn it.'

'It's not a big deal, is it?'

'Well, we do have a total stranger staying in my home this weekend and I really don't want them poking through my gym bag and sniffing my sports bra.'

He snorts a laugh at this. 'I told you already, it's an old lady, not some dirty old man. Relax. I'm sure she'll have better things to do than go looking through your smelly gym gear.'

The flippancy in his tone brings a ripple of tension to Anna's jaw. He doesn't get it. It's bad enough he's orchestrated this stupid house swap weekend, but the thought of not having her running gear with her... Anna shifts her bum, the cushion of the car seat long devoid of any comfort. Running helps with her anxiety, keeps her sane. But more importantly, it keeps her fast, keeps her prepared.

'Anyway, we're almost there.' Dan's hand squeezes her thigh and returns to the gearstick. 'There should be a turn-off coming up soon.'

Anna discreetly sighs out her frustration, then tries to coax some levity into her voice. 'I'm looking forward to seeing the place.'

The lie hangs in the air between them as she turns to stare out the passenger window, her breath blooming and fading on the glass. Above her, a flat dull sky stretches out like an old bed sheet that's seen better days. Anna's eyes scan the dormant landscape, all boggy fields and thorny hedgerows. Gnarled trees twist painfully into the late afternoon October air, stubborn leaves clinging defiantly to branches peppered with long-abandoned bird nests. A scrawny heifer watches her with doleful eyes as their solitary car trundles past. This road they're on is barely wide enough for two vehicles to pass each other, but that's okay: they've passed no other car for miles.

Any other woman would be delighted to be whisked away to a remote cottage for a romantic weekend. Dan's organised everything: it's their last weekend together before his visa expires and this time next week he'll be on his way back to Australia. At the thought of Dan leaving her, a familiar tightness begins to claw its way up from Anna's belly and grip at her chest. But she forces herself to swallow it back down. Right now, she needs to perk up, put on her happy face. She can't ruin his last weekend in

Ireland. God only knows, the past three months have been hell for Dan too.

Anna glances discreetly at her watch. It was only two hours ago that they closed the front door to her house in Skerries. But with every kilometre they've driven further from home, Anna's sense of disquiet has grown insistently louder. She shouldn't be here, acting like everything's fine. She should be at home in case the cops find something, in case they need her to come into the station. A romantic weekend away with a boyfriend to a cottage in the arse-end of nowhere is what a *normal* person does. But Anna Moriarty is not normal. Anna Moriarty is a *bad person*. As her mood begins to teeter, she busies herself with a quick rummage in her bag for a mint.

'You're sure we don't need to pick up anything before we arrive at the house?'

'Relax, love. I've packed everything we need.' Dan throws her his easy smile. 'The reviews say the house is well stocked. Danny Boy here has taken care of everything.' His hand rubs her knee again. 'I'm not completely useless.'

Anna moves her own hand to cup his knuckles and wonders if he can feel the cool clamminess on her skin. She would have preferred a hotel, but Dan insisted on using the house-swap website to find their accommodation. It will be more homely, he's told her, more relaxed than a stuffy hotel. But Anna knows the truth behind his decision — he's been diligently saving up his wages recently and this arrangement costs him nothing — so she'll bite her tongue. But the thought of staying in some random person's home, sleeping in a stranger's bed... Anna shifts in her seat again. What's really churning up her gut is the thought of that same stranger in Anna's home this weekend, rummaging through her stuff, unlocking windows, moving things. Anna takes her hand back. And as for the two cats... if anything were to happen to Nip and Tuck, she'd never forgive herself.

She closes her eyes against the bleak landscape and tells herself that everything is fine. She just needs to rein in her worries, focus on her breathing exercises.

*In for four…*
*Hold for seven…*
*Out for eight…*
*In for —*
'Jesus!'

Dan slams the brakes and blasts the horn. The car is on a tight bend and they've narrowly avoided hitting a sheep in the middle of the road. The animal has been tagged by its owner with red dye, and for a split second its damp wool looks like it's matted in blood. Dan crunches the gears again, curses under his breath and manoeuvres them around the sheep. He drums his fingers impatiently on the steering wheel.

'Now, where's this damn turnoff? Can you check your map?'

Anna taps her phone into life. Even after three months, the photo on her lock screen snags at her heart. A picture of herself and Ger, squeezed up close at a cafe table in a shaft of late April sunlight. Their heads touching, their eyes sparkling. Excited, confident, at ease, safe. Anna runs her fingertip gently over the pixels on the screen. Ger, with her big brown eyes, swarthy skin and hippy vibes, the unconventional lawyer with the heart of gold. Nothing like Anna, with her honeyed-blonde hair and her blue-green eyes. Best friends since school, closer than sisters. Anna smiles wanly at the photo. It's the same picture the cops used, Ger's face flashed onto TV screens across the country.

'Well?'

'What? Sorry. One sec, Dan.' Anna opens the map and zooms in. It takes a moment for her to see their position. 'Okay… did we pass a garage?'

'Yep, just now.'

'Okay, well, any moment you should see a...' Anna squints at the screen, '...a Meat Processing Plant? Is that another way of saying—'

'Abattoir, yeah. Or as I prefer, slaughterhouse.'

' *"Slaw da haus."* ' Anna mimics Dan's Aussie accent.

He slaps her playfully on the thigh. 'Ah to be sure, to be sure, my wee Irish leprechaun.'

It's good to see him smile. Maybe this weekend away is what they both need, after all.

Dan slows the car to a crawl and they look out Anna's window. An old abattoir, long abandoned and boarded up, sits decaying behind a sagging chain-link fence. Anna lowers her window and listens, but the place is devoid of human life. A faded sign for *'Cassidy's Meats'* stands at an angle in a bed of tall grass. Behind the sign, a weed-strewn car park sits pockmarked with shallow puddles of dirty water and smashed glass.

'Charming, Dan. Utterly charming.'

'Well, you can't say I don't take you to all the best places.'

A lone raven swoops past Anna's open window. Her heart jumps.

'Stupid bird. Shoo!'

Anna glares up at the bird as it eyeballs her with black pupils from atop the chain-link fence.

'This place gives me the creeps. Let's go, Dan.' She nods up the road, 'Our turn-off should be just up ahead on the right.'

A moment later, Dan turns the ancient Fiesta onto an even narrower side road. The car bumps along the lane, long tendrils of thorns dragging along the paintwork of the car.

'Watch out!'

He grabs Anna by the shoulder, yanking her back from the open window just in time. A whip of thorns flicks at the space where Anna's face was a second before. She quickly closes the window, then turns back to face him.

'Remind me again how you found this place?'

'I did a quick Google. Don't worry, Banana. Like I said, it's got great reviews, and the lady who owns the place has been doing house-swaps for years. She's a nice old dear. Trustworthy. She'll look after your house too.'

'You actually spoke to her?'

'Of course.'

Dan is shifting in his seat. From the little he's told Anna since he booked the place during the week, they'll be staying in a quaint cottage by ancient woods with a lake at the bottom of the garden. Nobody and nothing to disturb them.

'And she'll definitely be okay with Nip and Tuck?'

'Yes, love. I chose this house because her profile clearly stated that she loves animals. So Nip and Tuck will be well looked after.' He reaches the back of his hand up to Anna's cheek and presses it gently against her skin. 'So all you have to do is relax, okay?'

Anna turns her face and kisses the back of his hand. 'Okay.'

His skin smells good, his knuckles cool as marble against her cheek. Anna squeezes her eyes shut and tries to capture the moment. Dan will be on the plane back to Oz in just under a week, and Anna can't imagine how she's going to cope without him. He's been her rock over the past three months, more than she deserves. She'll save her tears until after he's gone.

'Check out the weirdo.'

'Hmm?' Anna follows Dan's gaze. A few metres away, on the other side of a rusted gate, a scruffy old man with a shock of thick white hair stands sharpening the end of a stick with a blade. He's wearing a stained brown suit belted with a piece of twine, a grubby tee-shirt, a pair of wellies and a flat cap. In the near distance behind him sits an old caravan. Near it, a clothesline hangs limply between two bare saplings, some yellowing undergarments flapping in the breeze. He must live here, Anna thinks. Somewhere out of sight, a diesel generator hums and sends up a filthy plume of smoke into the rapidly darkening sky. Anna's eyes return to the man. An expression of surly menace hangs on his craggy face. Anna's hand moves to the lock on her door.

'Lower your window, love.'

'What? No.'

'Go on. Quick, he's waiting. It's getting dark and I want to check if this is the right way.'

Anna lowers her window a few inches. Dan shouts across her.

'Hey mate. How's it going?'

Dan's foreign accent hangs loud and alien in the air between them. The old man says nothing but continues to slowly whittle the stick with his knife, his penetrating stare fixed on Anna. The methodical, insistent raspy slice of his blade continues. Dan shifts in his seat and tries again.

'Mate, are we near Laurel Cottage? Do you know the place?'

Anna has turned her face to look up the lane in front of them. Her cheeks are flushed and a prickle of sweat has broken out on her scalp. Dan is about to try again, but Anna's right hand comes to rest firmly on his thigh.

'Dan, let's go.'

Dan exhales, evidently irked at the stranger's stone-faced silence, embarrassed in front of his girlfriend. He glares at the weirdo as the car moves off, and mumbles something under his breath. Anna senses the mute man's gaze trailing after her, but she keeps her eyes fixed ahead.

Dan's big fingers fiddle at the dashboard, but he finds nothing but static on the radio. He slaps the dashboard, visibly annoyed at the man's rudeness, and the opening bars of the five o'clock news drift weakly up from the crappy speakers. He turns up the radio to fill the awkward silence. The newsreader's voice competes with the slap and scrape of gorse and blackberry cane along the sides of the car.

And suddenly Anna spots the house. The brambles thin out, and the narrow track opens up to a wide gate over a cattle grid. A weathered sign for *Laurel Cottage* has been hammered into the gate post. Dan pounds happily on the steering wheel, his relief palpable. Anna realises she's been gripping her seat and lets her body relax. Ahead of them, a short driveway curves up to a two-storey cottage which glimpses out at them from behind a dense cluster of laurel bushes, alder and oak trees. Dan hops out to open the gate, leaving Anna alone with the radio.

'... *and once again, following the attempted abduction of a woman...*'

Anna's hand darts to the volume button, her breath held.

'...*police have asked the public to be on the lookout for a white van with tinted windows. The driver of the van is thought to be male, white and around thirty years old...*'

Dan climbs back into the car, punches off the radio and starts whistling tunelessly to himself. As the car crunches up the short driveway, the newsreader's words echo in Anna's ears.

*A white van ... tinted windows.*

The familiar squeal of the brakes tugs at Anna's attention. Yet she sits for a moment, distracted, her thoughts galloping off through fields of guilt and remorse and the faintest hint of hope. The car is silent but for the ticking of its cooling engine. Beside her, Dan clears his throat. When Anna looks across to him, she notices new lines around his eyes which weren't there when she met him six months ago. He's looking older than his twenty-eight years. But there's something else in his eyes too at this moment, a pleading, of sorts. Anna understands. It's their last weekend together and he just wants to leave things on a high. A couple of nights away where they don't talk about what happened.

Dan nudges her with his shoulder and nods towards the cottage. 'Ready for your weekend to begin, Miss Moriarty?'

And in that moment, Anna decides to take the self-blame, the paranoia, her constant need to control, and to lock it all away for the weekend. For the next few days she'll dig deep, find a happy spark and blow some life into it. Bring back old Anna. She glances up at the house, then turns to flash her best smile at him.

'I couldn't be more ready, Mister Pell. Come on.'

# TWO

A WAVE OF STALE AIR hits them as Dan struggles the front door open. They're standing on the threshold, Dan holding a bag of groceries and a cool box full of chilled food. Beside him, Anna holds the key from under the front door mat. It takes a moment for their eyes to adjust to the gloom in front of them.

'Far out, did someone die in here?' Dan enters first, a scowl already darkening his face. He plonks the groceries and cool box on the kitchen island, then rubs his hands together, blowing on his fingers as he turns to survey the open-plan room. 'It's bloody freezing. You coming in, love?'

Anna has been hesitating at the door, a sixth sense holding her back. She's observing the annoyance on Dan's face as his eyes dart around the space. He'll be feeling responsible, like he's let her down, like he can't even organise a half-decent house for their last weekend together. Anna takes a deep breath of outside air and steps inside.

'It's cute! I like it.' Anna walks in, as breezily as she can muster. 'Why don't you light the fire and I'll bring in the rest of our stuff, yeah?' She clicks on a couple of lamps and tugs closed the heavy curtains, a stifle of dust swirling around her face. 'It's just a little rustic. We'll make it cosy in no time.'

Anna stands on tiptoe to kiss him, hoping it's not too late to navigate Dan away from an impending bout of moodiness. His arm comes around her, pulling her close, and Anna allows herself to melt into the embrace. She can't remember the last time they kissed like this. Dan's hand drifts down along her spine, over her waist, where it settles firmly against the curve of her jeans. Anna can see where this is going, and love him as she does, she won't be rutting on these filthy floorboards like a farm animal. She breaks away playfully.

'We'll save that for later, big boy. But right now, light the fire? It's baltic in here.'

Dan moons a sad face, but she can see the twinkle in his eye as he turns obediently to the stack of chopped wood by the hearth. While he busies himself at the fireplace, Anna steals a moment to take in her surroundings. Something's definitely off with this place. How on earth it would garner good reviews on a house swap website she does not know. It's not the furniture or decor, per se. That's just standard, if a little dated — a couple of dark leather sofas either side of a glass coffee table, a dark-wood dining table and six chairs, heavy curtains. No, it's something else. The sense that they weren't expected here. A frown creases Anna's forehead. She walks past the staircase and stops in a kitchen made up of old pine cabinetry. By the far bench top, a laminated page of instructions is attached to the wall. Anna scans it.

> *Welcome to Laurel Cottage!*
> *Instructions for recycling and waste...*
> *Tea, coffee, milk...*
> *Welcome basket of free-range eggs and organic bread in the fridge...*
> *Walk to lake...*
> *mobile phone number of owner...*

Her eyes track back over the laminated sign and stop on the *tea, coffee, milk* line. Great. A nice cuppa is just what she needs to warm up. And from her cursory glance earlier in the cool box, she doesn't think that Dan's brought milk.

'Dan, fancy a cuppa?'

Anna pulls open the door of the fridge and winces at the pong of stale air. The fridge is completely empty. She stands in the sickly yellow light of the fridge, her jaw tense, trying to calm herself in case Dan looks over. She thinks of her own cute cottage back in Skerries, and of the hours she spent this morning getting it shipshape. She pictures the two loaves she left in her breadbasket - one wholemeal, one gluten-free; the two cartons of fresh milk - one full-fat, one skimmed; the jam and butter, the basket of teas and the bag of coffee beans by her grinder; a dozen free-range eggs; fresh flowers and a welcome card by the bowl of fresh fruit. Her hand grips tighter on the greasy handle of the fridge door. She is livid.

'Will you stick some beers in the fridge for me?'

'Sure.'

As Anna shoves two six packs into the fridge, she glances up the staircase. God only knows what she'll find up there. To think she made up her own bedroom back in Skerries with brand new linens this morning. Even from here she can see a thin layer of dust on the dining table. How hard can it be to engage in a little bit of courtesy and basic cleanliness? It's like they've stumbled into a museum. Anna opens her mouth to ask Dan if he checked the reviews were recent, but he's humming away to himself over at the fireplace as the first twigs and kindling catch light. No, she'll not rock the boat. But whoever their 'host' is will be getting a pretty stroppy review at the end of the weekend. Damn sure.

Anna begins to unpack the groceries Dan brought for them. She was looking forward to a cup of tea and now she needs something in its place. She pulls out the bottles of red wine from the bottom of the grocery bag and twists one so that the label faces her.

*McLaren Vale Shiraz 2018.*

Anna bites distractedly on her inner cheek. In the past she'd have poured them both a generous glass already, would have gulped the frustration away. But no more. A drop hasn't passed her lips since Thursday 11th July. She needs a clear head, to be ready. And besides, she doesn't deserve to numb herself.

Fixed to the wall above the counter is a magnetic strip of chef's knives. Anna pulls the handle of the largest one and watches her reflection stretch and warp as she angles the steel blade in the lamp light. She glances over her shoulder to check Dan isn't watching her, then hovers the point of the blade over the tip of her index finger, feels its weight, tempting the sharp edge to pierce her skin. She imagines the slice, the focus, the release.

'What do you reckon's in here?'

Dan has come into the kitchen. Anna fumbles the knife back onto the wall holder with a metallic click. His hand is on a door Anna hadn't noticed. She turns to busy herself with the remaining groceries as the door rattles behind her.

'Dan!'

'What?'

'It says *'Private'*. And it's locked. Maybe that's meant to tell us something? How would you feel if our host went snooping around my house?'

He rolls his eyes, gives up on the locked door and guides Anna over towards the hearth where a fire has taken hold, the dry wood crackling and spitting. He regards her, smugly, and she laughs.

'Well done, Danny Boy. Fire-starter extraordinaire! Right, I'll get our bags in from the car.'

'I'll go, love. Relax.'

'No, you sit down. It's your weekend too. Back in a sec.'

As Anna reaches the front door, her hip grazes a small console table which holds a carriage clock, a pewter ashtray and the world's most ugly vase. The vase wobbles for a moment, before she rights it. She shakes her head at the tall monstrosity of coloured glass, a garish swirl of sickly hues, a rancid hangover from the seventies. There really is no accounting for taste.

Outside the sky has darkened, but no stars or moon are to be seen. The trees on the periphery of the land stand sombre, their trunks thickening into shadow on the ground. Anna pulls the front door closed behind herself to keep any heat from the fireplace inside. In the fast-fading remnants of twilight, the air is still. She squints into the gloom and pulls her jacket tighter around her body.

In the eerie chill, Anna's breath is visible. She walks quickly over to the car, glancing back to ensure Dan isn't looking out the window, then slides her phone from her jacket pocket. One steady bar of signal appears and she exhales a gentle sigh of relief. One bar of signal is all she needs. She'd feared that the cottage would be too remote, cut off from the outside world. But now she reminds herself that she's not living in one of those tropey suspense novels she used to read on the train to work. She stares at the phone for a moment, willing a message to appear from the cops, then slips it back in her pocket. She'll call Sergeant Rooney in the morning, chivvy him along. She's read how these things go: if you don't keep on top of the case, regularly pester the investigating officer, the files get discarded somewhere, and before long will be languishing in the bottom of some archive box in the bowels of a dusty basement. Anna has been like a dog with a bone these past three months, and, quite frankly, she doesn't give one hoot if the cops roll their eyes when they see her marching up the front path of the police station.

The boot creaks as she pops it to lift out their two weekend bags. She is about to slam it shut when she freezes. She spins around, her heart in her mouth. Her eyes dart towards the thick copse of alder trees near the driveway. Something moved in there. She's sure of it. A crack of wood. A rustle. She turns again, her chest pounding. The earlier words from the radio newscast play in her mind.

*A white van ... tinted windows.*

Could he have come for Anna too? She stands rigid, painfully alert, her breath a rapid rise and fall.

'Hello?' Her voice sounds piss-weak in the stillness. 'Is anyone there?' Her eyes strain in the dark, but the trees form a mass of indistinguishable shadow. She takes the smallest step forward.

'Banana, you okay?'

An oblong shaft of warm light has escaped the front door. Dan is beckoning her inside. Anna slams the boot and picks up their two bags.

'Just coming.' She walks quickly, pretending it's the cold air propelling her out of the darkness. She hurries into the refuge of the house and slams the door shut firmly with her heel.

# THREE

DAN PUTS DOWN HIS EMPTY BEER BOTTLE and drums his fingers on the bedroom windowsill. His other hand holds his phone close to his ear. She's not picking up. He fingers distractedly at the blind, but there's nothing but darkness outside the glass, and he lets the dusty slats snap back into place.

Anna's moving around downstairs, rustling up some dinner. He can hear her place the pot of water for the pasta on the stove. It was Anna who asked him to ring their host. Just a courtesy call, she'd said.

*Be nice*, she'd instructed him. *Just check she's in okay and that the cats are fed.*

Dan leans his arse against a low chest of drawers. The wizened leaves of a long-dead spider plant hang over the edge of the furniture. He tugs at the brittle leaves while the phone continues to ring in his ear.

'Come on. Pick up already.'

The sooner the old lady confirms everything's fine, the sooner Anna will relax. He saw the look on her face earlier, the disappointment when he opened the door to the house. She's pretending she's not bothered, but Dan knows Anna better than she knows herself. He'll have a subtle word with their host, Mrs Cassidy, if she ever answers her bloody phone.

Dan stands and paces out his frustration. The old woman must have arrived at Anna's house by now. No doubt she'll have her feet up on the sofa and the two cats will be happily sniffing around her belongings.

*Christ, if anything were to happen to Nip and Tuck...*

Dan doesn't even allow himself to finish that thought. Anna has become obsessive about Ger's two rescue cats. And now it's as if they've somehow come to embody Ger herself. The number of times he's almost killed himself tripping over them as they traipse around the house after Anna, in a constant state of being fed and cuddled and having their every need met. Dan can't even shoo them off the dining table these days without Anna spitting the dummy. He snorts quietly and shakes his head. He's jealous of two frigging rescue cats.

He glances at the screen of his still-ringing phone. It's definitely the number from the laminated sheet down in the kitchen. Now he's kicking himself that he organised this whole bloody weekend by messaging a stranger on a house swap website. He should have asked Mrs Cassidy for her phone number during the week. In hindsight it would have been smart to give her a quick call to make sure everything was legit. Oh well, too late now. He rubs the back of his scalp and wills the old woman to answer her damn phone. He scratches his nail across some dry skin on his lower lip. Maybe he should just tell Anna a little white lie for the sake of their collective sanity? Just say that the old woman made it into Anna's safely, and that the cats are fed and watered. What harm would it do? He'll give it another ten seconds.

'Dan?'

'One sec, love.'

*Come on. Answer.*

'Dan.'

He walks slowly to the bedroom door. Anna is coming up. He ends the call as she reaches the top stair. He opens his mouth, unsure yet if he's going to tell his white lie, but Anna speaks first.

'Ring her again.'

He frowns at Anna, noticing the distracted concern on her face. Anna has taken his elbow and is now guiding him down the stairs. He hits the redial button and they stop by the kitchen countertop. He goes to speak but Anna holds up a silencing finger. The pair of them stand mute, the only sound the crack and spark of the logs in the fireplace. Both stare off into the middle distance.

'Listen.' Anna's voice is a grave whisper. She has turned towards a shadowy corridor that neither of them has yet explored, and now Dan turns to face it too.

'Can you hear it?'

Anna tries the switch, but the light bulb is dead. Her other hand is on Dan's elbow again, a subtle tremor in her grasp. Dan can just about make out a single door at the end of the dark corridor. Now he is aware of a noise too, a pulsing sound. His feet move them slowly forward, Anna's breath shallow beside him. He reaches his hand to the door, the handle cold to the touch, and creaks it open. His fingers search for the light switch and a bare dusty bulb in the ceiling flickers to life. He's standing in the doorway of a small room, what looks like a basic office, containing a black leather chair and a desk with drawers. The walls are bare apart from some nails. Another dead plant droops over the edge of a pot on the corner of the desk. Dan moves slowly around the desk and carefully pulls open the two drawers, one at a time. Paperwork, files, pens and clips. Anna has moved towards the side of the desk and is peering at the slim space between it and the wall.

'Dan. Look.'

A mobile phone is plugged into the wall socket behind the desk. Anna sticks her hand in and retrieves it. She looks at its buzzing screen, then turns it towards Dan. His familiar number flashes back. He kills the call and they both watch as the phone in

Anna's hand dies. He risks a glance at Anna and sees a familiar worry line crease her forehead. She's gone a little pale.

'How do we contact her, Dan? How do we check the cats are okay? How do we—'

'Shh. Banana. It's fine.' He walks towards her, but she shrugs away his arm. 'She's an old lady. Probably doesn't use her phone much. She's probably just forgotten it. I do it all the time…'

Anna raises an eyebrow but says nothing. Dan has never forgotten his phone in his life. He watches as she forces out a slow exhalation.

'Look, I'll send her a message using the website. She was always quick to respond before.'

'I thought you'd spoken to her by phone?'

Anna's eyes are on him. He rubs the back of his scalp.

'Yeah, I did. Both. Phone and messaging using the website.' He swallows down the lie and turns to close the drawers, hoping to hide the redness flushing his face. 'Why don't I message her now. And you keep going with dinner?' He's aiming for casual, but he can hear a slight tightness in his own voice.

Anna has already headed back towards the kitchen, throwing a simple but firm *'Fine'* over her shoulder. As Dan bends down to close the lower drawer, he notices the corner of a photograph poking out from amongst the jumble of paperwork. He pulls it out and tilts it towards the bare bulb overhead. A middle-aged man in a suit smiles back at him. It looks like a dressy event, perhaps a wedding or a christening. A rough crease line runs down the side of the photo. As Dan unfolds the hidden half of the photograph, he puts out a hand to the desk to steady himself. A well-dressed woman stands cosily beside the man. Or, at least, it appears to be a well-dressed woman. The face and body have been sliced by a thousand tiny scores, her features obscured. Dan traces the tip of his index finger down the cuts in the photograph. He glances slowly around the small, cold room with its bare walls, as if that will make sense of what he's holding in his hand. But no answers appear. Beyond the desk, the window is uncovered, revealing the fathomless blackness outside. Dan makes eye contact with his own reflection and has a sudden sense of being watched. He folds the sliced woman back into her concealed position, slides the photograph back among the paperwork, then closes the bottom drawer. Not his concern, and definitely not something to mention to Anna... probably just some bored grandkid scratching with a nail or something.

'Dan, I'm serving up.'

As he turns to pull the door closed, Dan takes another glance at the fusty room. The whole property needs a good clean, multiple signs of long-term neglect apparent. He lingers for a moment, nibbling his bottom lip, and feels the first stirring of unease in his gut. He can't put his finger on it, but something isn't quite right with this place, and it's not just the dust, the dead plants or the forgotten phone. He flicks off the bare light bulb. And as he shuts the door, he bats away his disquiet, telling himself he's just a little tired after the drive. Everything's fine.

# FOUR

A SEA OF COLD MIST rolls over Anna's feet. It slithers around her ankles and somehow holds her rigid, rooting her to the spot. Her eyes dart around, an urgent need to know where she is. Slowly, through the breathing curtain of fog, the outline of forms come into focus. In front of Anna, ancient gravestones and Celtic crosses arise. And just beyond those, she sees the outline of an old church tower, long abandoned. She cannot tell if it's day or night, perhaps somewhere in between. But this place is familiar to her. She came here once with Ger. It's the cemetery, back in Skerries, but somehow different now. Any colour has been leached away, leaving Anna in a ghostly world the hue of aged bones. An eerie stillness hangs in the air around her. There is no birdsong, no hum of cars in the distance.

In front of her, the layers of grey thin, and Anna's gut tightens. A man is watching her. A cold fear paralyses her as the mist crawls further up her legs in greedy tendrils. All she can do is watch in horror as the man's form emerges into solidity. Anna opens her mouth, but no air will leave her lungs, the scream stolen before it escapes. No-one is coming to help her. She cannot see the man's face, his features obscured, but she's felt his presence before. For months he's been trailing her, lurking in shadowy corners, preparing to pounce.

Anna's panicked eyes lock onto the old church tower in the distance. If she could just make it there she might be able to barricade herself inside. She wipes her clammy hands on the legs

21

of her jeans and glances back at him. He's studying her, planning something, a cold determination in the set of his chin. The man has unfinished business.

An object glints by his side. It's a butcher's knife, and now Anna watches, transfixed, as he moves the blade slowly away from his body, then brings the tip of the knife into his right thigh. If it causes him pain, he does not show it. He repeats the action, slow and steady, deeper this time, the sickening slice and suck of his flesh the only sound in Anna's ears. And now he's moving towards her, his gait uneven, hobbling through the mist on his bloody leg. His knife is craving more.

With every ounce of strength she possesses, Anna pulls one foot, then the other, from the grip of the mist sucking at her ankles. And she runs. She runs like she's never run before. Her heart slams into her chest as she stumbles over graves, cutting her hands on hidden brambles and stones. But the old church tower seems no closer. She stumbles on in wild panic, a quick glance over her shoulder enough to tell her he is gaining on her. The knife continues to pierce his leg, the blade's surface now more blood than metal. When she reaches the tower she collapses against the thick oak door and bangs it with her fist. Splinters cut her hand and she pulls frantically on the heavy rusted knocker. The ugly sound of cutting flesh grows louder. Anna scrambles around the side of the tower, her back to the wall. Something black moves stealthily through the fog in front of her. It hangs like a black shadow in mid-air. And then, for the briefest moment, the mist thins and Anna sees a raven. She pushes her body away from the wall and turns. And she sees that she is no longer at the old church tower in the cemetery, but she's actually standing at the abandoned abattoir she drove past earlier with Dan. Anna leans her forehead against the wall, her eyes closed, her breathing still heavy. But utter relief courses through her veins. She laughs in the silence. It was just a dream. Her pounding heart starts to calm and a trickle of cold sweat runs down her spine. Behind her, the stupid raven caws from its perch on the fence, a gloriously normal sound in Anna's ears once more. She opens her eyes and notices a shadow flit across the wall in front of her face. The bird must be off. Anna turns to watch it disappear, but there is no bird. He has somehow followed her. The man raises his butcher's knife and brings the bloody blade down.

Anna screams herself awake. She sits bolt upright in the bed, her hand clutching her chest. Her eyes struggle to see through the gloom, and it takes her a confused moment to remember where she is. The cheap polyester bedsheets are drenched in her sweat and twisted around her legs. She kicks them off and swings her legs over the side of the bed, her jaw tense, her heart pounding. The same bloody nightmare has been tormenting her for months.

She exhales slowly and waits for her heartbeat to settle. A quick glance over her shoulder confirms that Dan's not beside her in the bed. She cocks her ear and hears the sound of his thunderous snoring coming up from downstairs. Earlier, she'd tried to rouse him from the sofa, but he couldn't be moved, his long limbs a dead weight, his open-mouthed face squashed against the cushions. On the coffee table in front of him had stood a second bottle of red, only an inch of wine remaining. And she'd seen the stubbed-out remnants of two joints in the ashtray by the back door. His snoring usually bothers Anna. But she listens now. There is comfort in its sonorous rhythm, as she sits alone in this unfamiliar bedroom.

*Everything is fine.*

She takes a sip of water from the glass on the nightstand and walks softly to the window, scrunching her bare feet against the roughness of the rug, a grounding into the here-and-now. The bedroom is at the back of the house and a break in the clouds allows the flinty moonlight to momentarily pick out the surface of the lake water in the background. Then, another cloud rolls across, and her view is plunged back into darkness.

Anna closes her eyes and listens. From the distance, a strange sound creeps into her awareness. There's something alive out there in the night, but it sounds like it's in pain. Probably just a stray cat in heat, she tells herself. Or a bird whose call is being weirdly reflected off the lake water. But the low guttural wail unsettles Anna, and her mind drifts back to the ghost stories her mischievous older cousins used to tell her to give her nightmares. She remembers tales of the banshee, a keening old woman with white hair and bloodshot eyes: to hear a banshee's demented cries foretold the death of a loved one before sunrise. Anna shakes away the childish memory, the lingering remnants of the nightmare stirring her overactive imagination. She's tired, she needs sleep. But as she climbs back into bed, the folklore follows her, an insistent whisper in the darkness.

*To hear a banshee means death for a loved one.*
*To see a banshee means death for oneself.*

Anna pulls up the blanket, shuts her eyes, and shimmies her body further down into the stranger's bed. She tuts at the silliness running through her mind. But minutes later, as she restlessly turns her body, one way, then the other, comfort continues to elude her. And Anna remembers she can no longer casually dismiss the notion of evil and monsters. Not after what happened to Ger.

# April

# FIVE

EVERY FEW SATURDAYS, Anna and Ger would jump on the morning train from Skerries into Dublin city centre, where Anna would head to the farmers' market in Temple Bar, and Ger would mooch around the vintage stores in and around George's Street Arcade. It was the first warm day of April, and with her eyes closed and her face tilted towards the sun, Anna listened in on the happy banter passing between the stallholders and their regulars at the market. The aroma of warm sourdough and fresh coffee permeated the air around her, and Anna pressed her lips together in anticipation of the crepe she'd just ordered. She could eat whatever the hell she wanted today because herself and Ger had been for their swim earlier. That morning, like every other Saturday morning, Anna's bedroom door had received a no-nonsense knock at eight sharp.

*Come on, you. A quick dip will do you the world of good.*

And Ger had been right, of course. That morning's swim, like all the others before, had blasted away the cobwebs and left Anna buzzing. The whole swimming thing had started off as a bit of joke — or so Anna had thought — when Ger had gifted her a pair of neoprene booties. But Ger had been serious, bending Anna's ear on the benefits of cold-water swimming, until Anna had begrudgingly relented. So every Saturday, for the past year or so, they'd hobbled across the stony shore of the North Strand at Skerries, come rain or shine, and threw themselves into the purifying sting of the Irish Sea. Their screams and whoops would pierce the air, the two women scudding freezing water at each other, before fully submerging themselves in the icy prickle. Afterwards, there'd always be an unladylike stumble across sharp stones to their bags, and the urgent rummage for a beach towel, saltwater dripping, hair plastered to foreheads, passers-by nodding in silent admiration as excited dogs strained to join the two grinning friends. That post-dip high was the best.

'Anna. Dark chocolate and banana.'

Anna blinked herself back into the sunny market square, then turned to find Camille, the elderly French stallholder, holding out her crepe on a paper plate with a little bamboo fork.

'Merci, Camille. A bientot!'

As the old lady turned to serve another customer, Anna shuffled backwards to her sunny spot near the corner of the market square. Ger would be waiting at the cafe up the road already and Anna didn't want to be late. Something had recently started to trouble Anna's housemate and Anna didn't want to cause Ger even the smallest amount of additional stress. But right now, Anna just needed to steal a moment to herself, to savour the crepe, to feel the sun on her skin. Just one glorious minute. Anna moved the fork through the molten chocolate and spiked a generous piece of crepe. And right at that moment, something slammed into her back. The plate and its contents flopped onto the ground.

'Oh...shit. I'm sorry about that.' From behind her, a man's voice. Foreign.

Anna looked at the mess on the ground, then over to the crepe stall where a queue had now formed. She'd have no time to order another one.

*Damn it.*

The man's shadow shifted awkwardly beside her and Anna turned to give the clumsy oaf a piece of her mind. She had to look up to meet his eye. The man standing shamefaced in front of her was boyishly handsome, around six-two, with short dark hair and chocolate-brown eyes. He watched her with an uncertain smile, as his hand rubbed the back of his scalp. Anna's eyes did a quick and subtle rove downwards. The top three buttons of his short-sleeved shirt were open against the warmth of the day and the strap of his backpack had tugged against the material to reveal a glimpse of toned chest, lightly sprinkled with dark hair. Anna forced her eyes up towards his face again. The poor guy looked embarrassed as all hell.

'I'm *really* sorry about that.'

She picked up the accent now. Australian.

He was bending to clean up the mess, but old Camille had spotted it and was shooing him off as she took charge with her broom.

'Can I buy you another one? It's the least I can do.'

His embarrassment had faded and there was a directness to his handsome gaze now. Anna felt slightly bashful and a flush of heat rushed up from her chest. She feigned interest for a moment in Camille's stall so that she could hide the pink in her cheeks.

'Look, it's fine. It was just an accident.' She turned to leave. 'Well, have a good—'

'I'm Dan.'

She stopped, turned back. The man's gaze was playful, tempting, daring her to look away.

'Hi Dan.' A momentary pause. 'I'm Anna.'

They shook hands, the touch lingering, and the hubbub of the marketplace faded into the background.

'So, you're Australian?'

'Sure am. From a little country town in New South Wales.'

'Anywhere near Sydney?'

'Just over six-hours on a good day. So, not far by Aussie standards. And what about you – are you a *Dub*?'

Anna laughed. 'God, no. But I've lived in Skerries for years.'

He looked at her blankly.

'Sorry. Skerries is a seaside town in North County Dublin. All seagulls and stony shoreline. Good seafood restaurants and decent pubs. It's cute. But I'm a blow-in, originally from Drogheda.'

That blank look again.

She laughed. 'It's a town just up the road, about an hour from here.'

Anna's phone pinged in her back pocket. Ger would be wondering where she was.

'Sorry. I actually have to be somewhere.' Anna's feet made no sign of moving. 'I'm meeting someone.'

The man adjusted the backpack over his shoulder. 'Well, it was nice nearly getting to know you, Anna from Drogheda.'

'You too, Dan, from six hours outside Sydney. Well. Bye then.'

Anna forced herself to turn this time, sensing his eyes on her back as she merged in with the crowd. She walked on, fighting the desire to glance over her shoulder. It was only as she exited the market square onto Essex Street that she realised she was heading in completely the wrong direction.

*Jesus, Anna. A cute guy gives you a bit of attention and you get all flustered.*

She skirted around the groups of ambling tourists and buskers and picked up her pace as she turned up Eustace Street. Then she stopped abruptly on the cobble stones. He was exiting through the arch on the side of the Square and was now only two metres in front of her. He looked in her direction.

'Oh. Hello, stranger.'

'Dan. Long time no see. What's new?'

He grinned, then took a step towards her, so that they stood in tight, as people flowed around them. Anna felt the heat radiating from his body, smelt the woody base-note of his aftershave. She wanted to lean in closer.

'Won't he mind?'

'Won't who mind what?'

'Your boyfriend. You're going to be late…'

Anna smirked and glanced down the street, stalling.

'Actually, I'm meeting my housemate, Ger.'

'Ger? Oh right. Short for Gerry?'

'Ger's short for Geraldine. But the last person who called her that is chained to a rock at the bottom of the Liffey.'

'I see. So, there's no …'

She looked off down the street once more, painfully aware of the bashful grin on her face. She was out of practice at this flirting malarkey. 'No, there's no…'

His look was hungry and Anna surprised herself by holding his gaze.

She cleared her throat. 'Why don't you join us? Myself and Ger can show you some Irish hospitality. Tell you all about Leprechauns and the Blarney Stone.'

The invitation was out of Anna's mouth before she could stop it. This random guy could be a serial killer. For all she knew there was a severed head in the backpack casually slung over his shoulder. Inwardly, Anna rolled her eyes and instructed her overcautious self to shut up for once.

'Really? Won't your housemate mind?'

'She'll mind if I'm late.' Anna glanced at her watch. 'Which I officially now am.' She took a few steps up Eustace Street, then turned to face him, naughty and spirited. 'Well… are you coming then?'

The man laughed, shook his head and sauntered after her.

# SIX

ANNA STOOD IN THE DOORWAY of the bustling cafe and scanned the tables of weekend brunchers. There was Ger, sat over at the far corner, a lovely buttery light streaming in the window to the right.

'Is she here?'

Anna turned to Dan and nodded. 'Yep, follow me.'

As they skirted their way around busy tables and weaved around efficient waitstaff, Anna had a sudden urge to kick herself. She'd just met a new man mere minutes ago, and now, here she was, about to introduce him to her stunning housemate. What the hell had she been thinking? It wasn't as if Anna, herself, was a bad-looking girl — she'd rate herself a decent 8.5 out of ten — it was just that Ger was next level, a straight-up ten. And the worst part was, Ger didn't seem to care about or even notice her own looks. Any other woman with Ger's dark beauty and shapely figure would have oceans of notions about herself. But not Ger. And maybe that's what seemed to send men in her orbit a bit doolally. Even as they approached her, Anna noticed the sly glances of a handsome young lad at a neighbouring table. But Ger was lost in the Irish Times crossword, nibbling the end of her pencil as her thick dark hair cascaded down over her bare honeyed arms. An empty coffee cup sat atop a messy spread of weekend supplements in front of her.

Anna dropped her bag onto an empty chair and began to shrug off her denim jacket.

'Sorry, Ger...'

'Ah, there you are. I was wondering—' Ger hesitated on spotting the stranger hovering behind Anna. Her gypsy eyes hopped back to her best friend, her eyebrow arched. 'Did you get a little... distracted?'

'Ger, this is Dan.'

Ger stood, big smile, hand out.

'Dan? Nice to meet you. Are you joining us?' She glanced to Anna, a wordless dance, then motioned to a spare seat. 'Please...'

Dan slipped off his backpack and hung it over the back of the chair. 'If that's alright? I don't wanna intrude.'

'No, you're grand.' Ger folded up the newspaper and stuffed it into her tote, then settled herself back into her seat. 'So, I'm guessing you're not from around these parts. Have you been here long?'

Anna sat quietly. Poor unsuspecting Dan was about to get the third degree.

'I've been travelling for a year and a half but just arrived in Dublin a few days ago. I thought I'd give the city a go before my visa expires and I have to return to Oz.'

'And your first impressions?'

Ger's leg nudged Anna's under the table.

'So far, so good. Bloody pricey though. Can't believe how much it costs to rent a room here. I'm staying at a hostel until I get settled somewhere for the next few months.'

'You should move further out. Somewhere on the train line. Like us.'

'Oh yeah?'

As Anna and Ger filled Dan in on various Dublin suburbs and their pros and cons, an efficient waitress with a wild mop of red hair leaned in for Ger's coffee cup. She returned within a minute with their order, three cold bottles of cider. The trio filled their glasses and toasted. Anna took a long, delicious swig from her glass and settled back into her seat.

Ger nodded across the table. 'So, Dan, I'm guessing with those shovels you're not a concert pianist?'

Dan laughed and lifted his right hand, examining the lines and pads of his palm in the shaft of afternoon sunlight. Perhaps it was the half glass of cider on an empty stomach, but Anna found her left hand rising to meet this relative stranger's, her palm pressing gently to his, her fingers instantly dwarfed by his. Anna startled herself with her sudden intimacy and she withdrew her hand back to the table.

'I do whatever I can. Grew up on a farm, but I'm mostly labouring while I travel. Plenty of work on the building sites and the money's decent.' Dan placed his hand back on the table and turned his attention to the woman beside him.

'And Anna from Drogheda. How do you make a living?'

Anna inwardly winced, her voice low. 'I'm a Financial Adviser. It's really not very interesting.'

'Anna makes rich people richer,' Ger added. 'She knows tax legislation backwards and is the queen of nudging the rules within an inch of breaking them.'

Anna shifted in her chair. In the past couple of years, she'd become increasingly sensitive about her job. She was damn good at what she did — always did have a head for numbers — and her colleagues at *Houghton, Hartery & Lynch* were pleasant, if not a little uptight. But it wasn't what she'd envisaged doing with her time on earth. Sometimes she'd look at Ger, watch her doing pro bono work in the evenings, hear her talk excitedly about someone else she'd helped to get back on their feet, and Anna would wonder how nice it would be to truly make a difference where it was needed. But in those moments, when she'd toy with the idea of making a leap into something more rewarding, she'd find herself focusing only on the risks involved. And before she knew it she'd be reminding herself about her regular salary, the easy commute and the comfort in the familiarity of her days. And just like that another month would pass and her rich clients would be a little bit richer.

'A smart cookie, hey?' Anna hadn't noticed, but Dan's hand had come to rest beside hers on the table, and now his pinkie was gently nudging hers. Her own finger held its position for a moment, then with a barely perceptible pressure pressed back against his.

'Shit!'

Ger's face had paled and she was sliding down in her seat. Anna followed her friend's gaze. Only a couple of metres away, none other than Gavin Sweeney, stood outside the window, his phone pressed to his ear.

'Oh shit!' Anna ducked in beside Dan's shoulder.

'Please don't look this way,' Ger whisper-begged, 'Please don't look this way…'

Now Dan was staring out the window. 'Who is he?'

'It's Ger's boss. Gavin. Bit of a dickhead.' Anna peeked cautiously out from behind Dan's bulk at the stocky little ferret-faced man barking into his phone. Anna had only met him a couple of times in the past, but since his promotion a few months ago the guy was moving with a touch more swagger. If he was chocolate he'd eat himself.

Ger leaned cautiously forward on the table, her hand up to shield the side of her face closest to the window. She whispered over to Dan, 'We started at the law firm on the same day. Fast forward two years and he gets the promotion that I was gunning for. Anyway, he became my manager in January and now—'

Ger stopped talking, abruptly sat back. Outside the window, Gavin had turned to face them. Anna found herself holding her breath. Gavin was leaning in closer to the window, straining to see. Suddenly, he bared his teeth and lifted a finger to his mouth.

He dug out a small fleck of broccoli from between two of his upper teeth, frowned at it, then flicked it onto the pavement. Anna snorted a laugh, then noticed the pained expression on Ger's face. Back outside, Gavin smiled at his reflection in the window, then turned and walked off, a slight unevenness to his gait.

'Did he hurt himself?' Dan's attention trailed after the man.

Anna exhaled in relief and Ger knocked back the rest of her cider.

'He has one leg shorter than the other,' said Ger, placing her empty glass back down. 'I don't know what happened, but one of the lads in the office made a snide comment behind Gavin's back one day, not long after the promotion. Called him Sniper's Nightmare. Gavin found out and the guy was gone within days.'

Anna shuffled herself into a more upright position on her chair. 'I'm actually pretty sure I saw him not far from our road one night. And the thing is, he lives miles away. But he's started drinking in one of our locals. Bit of a stalker, if you ask me.' Across the table, Ger bristled. Anna could have kicked herself. 'Sorry, Ger.'

'Anyway.' Ger cleared her throat and lassoed the topic back again. 'He's harmless. He just asks me to work late sometimes, hangs around, can pester me a bit, you know?' Ger ran a finger down the side of her glass. 'He must just be a little smitten with yours truly. Can't really blame him, can I?'

Ger's laugh sounded hollow, and when Anna glanced at her friend, there was a tiredness behind the wan smile. There was nothing harmless about the likes of Gavin Sweeney. The condescending gobshite was undermining Ger's every move at work, and consequently, her confidence had been knocked. It was as if someone had turned the colour down on Ger so she was now a washed-out version of her once vibrant self. Anna hated the guy. She knew his type well. A classic gas-lighter, full of charm

35

and utterly believable. In a swift movement, Anna hopped off her seat and jumped in beside Ger, draping an arm around her best friend's shoulder.

'We'll figure it out, okay?'

'Thanks, hon. It's fine. Really.' Ger paused, then fixed Dan with a fierce look. 'I love this woman. And I'll cut the balls of any bloke who treats her badly.'

Dan's mouth opened, but no words came out, and after a split-second the two women burst into spirited laughter.

'Sorry, Dan. Only messing with you.' Ger struggled to speak through the sudden laughter. 'Or am I?'

The friends' mirth drew attention from the surrounding tables.

'Don't move!' Dan grabbed Anna's phone from the table and pushed his chair back a little.

'Okay, ladies. Say cheese.'

Anna and Ger sidled in closer to each other, their heads touching, and beamed their best smiles to the phone lens. Dan took the shot, then examined his handiwork.

'That's a beaut. Definitely a keeper. Look.'

The two friends leaned towards the phone, their brows creased as they scanned the image. Anna realised she was expecting to see a version of herself which was too puffy, or shiny, or taken from the wrong angle. But for once her inner critic lay silent. Dan was right. It *was* a great shot, with something timeless about their smiling faces in the warm hue of the afternoon sunlight. It was a keeper, alright. Best friends forever, their whole lives ahead of them.

Dan stood and winked at Anna, then headed off wordlessly to the bar to get them another round. Anna leaned her head against Ger's shoulder.

'Well, I'm dying to hear. What do you think of him?'

A silence extended. Anna sat up and turned to face her friend. Ger's smile from a moment ago had evaporated and now a frown line creased her brow. She was staring vacantly out to the street, her eyes focused on the middle distance, as a single tear tripped down her cheek. Anna put her arm around Ger's shoulder again, feeling useless as her friend continued to slowly unravel.

*No*, thought Anna, *there was absolutely nothing harmless about the likes of Gavin Sweeney.*

# October

# SEVEN

ANNA IS ON THE BOTTOM STAIR pulling on her shoes.

'You sure you won't come for a quick walk?'

Dan's response is a woeful groan. He's at the kitchen table, a crease line down his face from where he slept on the sofa last night. He takes another tentative sip of his Bloody Mary, then lays his head back down carefully on his forearms. Anna pulls on a light rain jacket, then rubs the back of his scalp. She leans in to kiss his stubbly cheek.

'Did someone have a bit too much fun last night?'

A caustic belch escapes Dan's mouth. Anna jumps back.

'Ah Dan. Gross. You need to brush your teeth.' She glances around the room. It's no less miserable in the light of day, and now the whole place stinks like a brewery. She opens the back door and turns to look at him over her shoulder.

'I won't be long. Maybe we'll go out for a spin later? Find a pub for lunch?'

A non-committal grunt from the table. Anna lets herself out into the back garden and takes in a deep lungful of fresh air.

The day is overcast, but so far it's dry, and she spends a moment taking in her surroundings. In front of her, at the end of the scruffy back garden, is the start of a curving path, guarded on either side by a thick cluster of scraggly old rowan trees. Anna walks slowly towards the path, her eyes scanning the shadowy spaces between the trees. These days, everywhere she looks, she can't help but sense threat and danger. She's been like this since that night in July, her confidence in the world shaken. But there's nothing to fear here, she reminds herself. As she steps into the shadows, a faint echo of a disturbing dream momentarily pulses in the depths of her memory — a misty cemetery, a keen blade, a frantic need to run — but just as quickly it's gone again. She zips up her jacket against the cool, dank air, forces her shoulders back and picks up her pace. A moment later she veers to her left. She'll save the lake for later, but right now she needs to put distance between herself and the house. At a barbed wire fence marking the perimeter of the back garden, she glances back to confirm Dan's not watching her from one of the windows. She pushes down the top strand of rusty wire with her hand, slowly swings her leg over to straddle it, then sweeps her other leg carefully across. She wades through knee-high grasses, picking up a thin birch switch to swipe and slash the stinging nettles in her way.

As she moves further from the house, familiar thoughts begin to clamber for air, Ger never far from her mind. Anna exhales a long, slow sigh. It's the not knowing what happened to Ger which eats away at Anna the most. Ger could be drugged and catatonic on a filthy mattress somewhere, chained to a basement wall, her throat long raw from unwitnessed screams. Such dark thoughts aren't new — Anna must have worked through every permutation and combination of what might have befallen Ger, to the extent it all seems to play like nonstop white noise in the back of her brain. A complicated dance of grief and guilt has left her worn out, layer over layer over layer, compressing and calcifying inside her, a hard pointed knot now taking up permanent residence in that delicate space between her stomach and her heart. But one thought she simply won't entertain is that Ger is dead. Ger is alive out there somewhere, waiting to be found. She simply has to be. It's this thought alone that forces Anna out of bed each day, that cajoles her to put one foot in front of the other. She must never give up hope.

The further she moves from the lake, the higher she climbs, and after a couple of minutes her body has heated up under her jacket. She unzips it as she circles around a low thicket of bush, then stops abruptly. She has arrived at the edge of an old quarry. A drop of about twenty metres lies just in front of her. She shuffles closer, leaning carefully over the edge. Below is a pool of murky brown water, pocked with boulders of various sizes. On the far side of the base of the quarry are the blackened remnants of a campfire. A few faded tags of graffiti on some of the lower boulders near the waterline are the only other signs of human visitation over the years. There is no access road evident, any tracks long reclaimed by nature. Beyond the quarry the trees thin and give way to ragged fields, the old stone walls a testament to the hands that built them in centuries past. A few farm sheds and outbuildings strew the distant landscape. Anna looks to the horizon where brooding cloud hangs off to the West, no doubt brewing up a storm for later. Apart from the gentle breeze sifting through the grasses behind her, there is no sound whatsoever.

She reminds herself why she's here, taking out the phone from her pocket, making a mental note of the slightly better signal from up here. Sergeant Joe Rooney answers on the first ring.

'Anna Moriarty. And how are you on this fine day?'

Anna looks off to the distance. Down the line she can hear him take a sneaky suck on his vape. He keeps it in the top drawer of his desk at the station, where a framed picture of himself, his Italian wife and their two olive-skinned teenage daughters sits proudly near a never-ending mess of paperwork. There's still a croak of morning in his voice.

'I'm grand, Joe.' Anna sweeps a loose strand of hair out of her eyes. It still feels weird calling Sergeant Rooney by his first name. But he'd insisted, a week into opening the missing person's file on Ger. The man has seen Anna at rock bottom, snotting into his handkerchief, all wild hair and mascara-streaked cheeks. But still, it feels too informal.

He slurps his coffee and starts typing something into his computer. 'So, no news, Anna, since we last spoke. I would have—'

'Did you hear about the abduction? The white van with tinted windows?'

Anna hears the tight neediness in her words, a desperation for Joe Rooney to get on board with her theory. He's pausing, another long draw on his vape. The man must rue the day he ever gave Anna his personal mobile number.

'I did hear about that one, yes.' He's tentative, working out how best to handle her. 'But it's not enough to establish a pattern...'

'But—'

'This was an *attempted* abduction. The young woman fought him off. One white van with tinted windows three months after Ger disappeared ... well, as I said, it's not really a pattern, is it?'

Anna closes her eyes, willing him to not ignore this. There *has* to be a link. In the background she can hear the squeak of his desk chair as he sits back, no doubt rubbing a hand down his tired face. He's a decent man, but sometimes Anna wants to slap him out of his stupor, shake him into action.

'But it's too much of a coincidence to be overlooked. Don't you think—'

'Anna, listen to me. I want to find Ger as much as you do. And I've promised you before that I won't stop until we find out what's happened to her. But right now, all we've got is a white van with tinted windows, the driver of which tried and failed to abduct a young tourist the other night down in County Wexford.

This is three months after Ger vanished in a different location. And besides…'

Anna opens her eyes and stares unblinkingly at the storm clouds in the distance. She knows what's coming. He's clearing his throat, preparing to soften his next words.

'And besides, you were the only person to mention the white van the night of Ger's disappearance. No other witnesses saw it. We looked into it at the time, but still have no leads. It's likely just a coincidence. Nothing more.'

Anna has a sudden urge to fling her phone at the quarry boulders down below. To watch it shatter and splinter into a million different pieces.

'Anna?'

She can't speak. She knows she needs to work with this man, but right now, there's an animal fury in her which wants to cause him serious harm.

'Anna, I've got another call coming in. I'll be in touch if there's any developments.'

The call dies in her ear. Anna stands, immobile for a moment, her gaze on the middle distance. Her throat is dry as she swallows, her jaw clenched, a familiar rigidity in her shoulders. But something else is pushing up from her core in that moment. Bubbling up from a deep well, rolling through her, wavelike, is the start of a terrible realisation, something that's been lingering on the outskirts of her awareness for a while now: Anna's on her own. The cops are beginning to focus elsewhere, their interest in this case waning faster than she'd feared. This shouldn't surprise her. The media lost interest long ago, why should the cops be any different? Even Anna and Ger's friends appear to have checked out recently. Anna's noticed them watching her with a pained wariness when they cross paths in the village, all furrowed brows and patronising arm rubs, as if Anna's unceasing search for her best friend is a burden which Anna, alone, must carry. They tolerate her now, walk on eggshells around her. But worst of all, they've given up hope.

A fat tear runs down her cheek and Anna wipes it away impatiently with the heel of her hand. In a few days' time she'll be losing Dan as well. The timing could not be worse. She's frightened when she pictures herself, this time, next week, alone at her house with the two cats and her maudlin thoughts. How in hell will she cope without him? She has a sudden urge to lie down right now and curl in on herself, to fall asleep here amid the dewy grass and damp earth and shut the world away. Let someone else take care of everything. She is pure exhausted from carrying this thing on her own. And in that instant, by a quarry's edge in the middle of nowhere, Anna feels more alone that she's ever felt in her life.

She turns and looks across to the roof of the Cassidy house, the tiled outline just visible through the cluster of surrounding trees, and pictures Dan cradling his hungover skull at the table. She sighs into the wind. It's at times like this that she'd love to rant to Dan, to just unleash everything, to be heard. But the poor guy has his limits too. Six months they've been together. And in the three months since Ger vanished, he's bent over backwards to support Anna as best as he knows how. She thinks of the countless times he's encouraged her to eat, how he's coaxed her out of her sweatpants and into the shower, the mornings he's wrapped her up and forced her out for brisk walks along the coastline. Those days are gone, though. Now, the topic of Ger rankles him. It's not that he doesn't care — Dan and Ger got on like a house on fire since that afternoon Anna introduced them in the cafe — but he finds Anna's theories more and more outlandish and exhausting. She knows he wants nothing but the best when he tries to steer her back towards some semblance of normality. He sees the toll this is taking on her, how she's unravelling into a husk of her former self, but his patience is wearing thin. Anna turns and kicks a loose rock towards the edge of the quarry ledge. She hasn't made it easy on him. She's too quick to anger nowadays, adept at rounding on him and pushing him away as if it's all his fault.

When Dan leaves on Thursday, she'll drive down to Wexford, ask around about this latest attempted abduction. Keep her brain distracted. Do the cops' job for them. Why the hell not? It's not like she could make things worse. She looks down at the small rock by her foot and shakes her head. People are useless. That's the cold, hard reality. Until Ger is found, Anna will rely solely on herself. With the toe of her shoe, she nudges the rock over the edge and watches it drop and splash in the shallows below, instantly swallowed by the murk.

One evening, three months ago, Anna let Ger walk home alone from the pub. But Ger never did make it home. And now Anna has to live with the consequences of that selfish choice. No matter how wretched she feels, she has one job to do now. She's going to find Ger and bring her home. And maybe — maybe, then — she'll begin to think about forgiving herself.

Anna glances around the bleak landscape. Her eyes trail the overgrown laneway of thorny brambles down to the turn-off, then trace the main road until she catches glimpses of the sagging chain-link fence and the abandoned abattoir. Her gaze washes over the rolling fields, towards low hills and the way back home. She stands tall and sucks in a deep lungful of cool air, a subtle stirring within, as her fingers curl in towards her palms.

Someone out there took Ger. And Anna will do whatever it takes to find the bastard. Even if it kills her.

# EIGHT

DAN'S UPSTAIRS IN THE SHOWER, his croaky baritone competing with the fizz of the water. The kettle is just coming to a boil when Anna's phone rings. It's her neighbour from home: lovely, bighearted Juliette from down the lane. Forty-five, divorced, twin boys, always knitting, and forever failing to control her rowdy pack of muddy Labradors.

'Hey Juliette.'

'Hiya Anna. You alright? You sound a bit flat.'

Anna grabs the least chipped mug from a row of hooks on the wall and drops in a tea bag.

'No, I'm grand. Sorry.' She lowers her voice even though the shower is still running. 'It's just this place Dan booked, well, it's a bit shite, if I'm honest.'

'Oh, that's a shame. Well that's kind of why I'm phoning. I know you're doing that house swap thingy…'

'Yeah?'

'Well, I stayed down in my Mam's last night and came back up this morning. Anyway, as I was passing your place a few minutes ago, I thought I'd pop in to check if your Mrs whatshername—'

'Cassidy.'

'Mrs Cassidy, yeah, needed anything.'

Bless Juliette. Any excuse to stick her nose in. At the fridge Anna inwardly curses as she remembers there's no milk. Damn it, she'll have her tea black.

'That was very thoughtful. And?'

'Well, she's parked up on your driveway. But when I knocked on the door there was no reply.'

'Right, well, she probably just walked into the village or went for a stroll along the beach or whatever. Maybe just let her be?'

'Well, that's the thing. I'm pretty sure I saw someone through the frosted glass of your front door. Just standing at the end of your hallway. When I bent down to look in through the letterbox they'd disappeared.'

Anna winces as she imagines Juliette bellowing in through the letterbox, bothering the old woman. No doubt Mrs Cassidy just wants some peace and quiet.

'You're very considerate, Jules, but I think she's used to her own company. She even left her phone here, so I reckon she's a little scatty too. But look, as long as she hasn't burnt the house down, then I'm happy enough.'

A small hesitation on the line. Anna stares out the kitchen window, waiting.

'I could try again later? When I take the dogs for a walk?'

'It's fine, Jules. She probably just likes her own space?'

'Whatever you like.' A curt coolness has crept into Juliette's tone.

'Listen, Jules, you're a real pal. I appreciate it. I do. But we'll be back tomorrow afternoon. How's about I pop over to you then for a cuppa and I can fill you in on all the goss.'

A resigned sigh down the phone. 'I suppose so.' Another pause. 'I might make a lemon drizzle.'

'I don't deserve you, Jules. See you tomorrow.'

Anna hangs up and picks up the kettle. She's about to pour boiled water for her black tea when she notices a build-up of grimy tannin on the inside of the chipped mug. She has a sudden urge to pick up the filthy mug and fling it at the far wall. This place is an absolute kip. And here she is, worried that her guest shouldn't be disturbed. Anna once again thinks of the effort she went to for this bloody Mrs Cassidy, leaving her own kitchen well-stocked, ensuring her own house was sparkling. She puts the kettle back down and turns towards the musty living room. Dan's tone-deaf singing taunts her from the shower upstairs. Anna could kill him. Why on earth he chose this depressing hovel for their last weekend together... She walks over to the sofa and plonks her backside down on the lumpy cushion.

During the week she'd specifically asked Dan if he'd checked the reviews on this place. *Of course*, he'd promised her. *Relax*, he'd said. *Don't you trust me?*, he'd countered with hurt eyes. How could he have got it so wrong? On the coffee table in front of her sits Dan's laptop. Anna stares, unblinking, for a moment. It wasn't just reviews of the house Anna had been wanting to know about. It was reviews on their host, as well. Right now, a stranger currently has free rein to rummage around Anna's home. And, more importantly, this Mrs Cassidy is responsible for minding Ger's two cats as well.

The fizz of the water upstairs has stopped, the pipes shuddering back to silence. Anna's eyes are fixed on the laptop. She'll be quick. She snatches it from the coffee table, drumming her fingers as she waits for it to fire up.

*Come on.*

In the browser, she opens Dan's history. She clicks the first result in the drop-down list, then frowns as she leans forward. It's strange to see a picture of this very room she's now sitting in. It's the same, but so very different. She enlarges the first image. Fresh flowers sit in a vase on the coffee table. A bowl of fruit and a welcome bottle of wine adorn the kitchen counter. She clicks through other images: the version online looks homely and warm. Anna minimizes the gallery and scrolls to the reviews section. Her eyes scan quickly, her breath held, as she readies herself to stumble upon something dodgy. But everything is positive. In fact, better than positive. The reviews are all stellar.

*'Such a warm welcome.'*
*'A truly wonderful rural retreat'*
*'Amazing host.'*
*'Best weekend ever.'*
*'Spotless!'*

Anna looks off to the corner of the room and chews on the inside of her cheek. Was this the same property? She looks back at the website and then scrolls to the top of the *Reviews* section. She clicks the *Sort* button to reorder the results and leans in closer to the screen. The most recent review is roughly one year old. Anna slumps back against the sofa. There is nothing for this year and it's already October. Maybe Mrs Cassidy had been ill or was overseas for a while and couldn't do house swaps. Anna softly closes over the laptop and tries to ignore the little sense of disquiet which is awakening in the back of her skull. Something just doesn't add up.

Two hands grab Anna's shoulders. She leaps out of her skin.

'Shit, Dan! You scared the life out of me.'

Dan leans over the back of the sofa to nuzzle Anna's neck. He smells fresh, a million times better than he did this morning. With one hand he whips his laptop out of Anna's hands.

'Naughty, naughty. Are you logging in to check your work emails? No work this weekend, Banana. You're on holiday. All those wealthy tax dodgers can just wait.'

He dances away behind her, and Anna has a sudden fear he'll open the laptop. If he does he'll know straight away that she doesn't trust him to organise a simple weekend away. They'll row and the weekend will be ruined. Anna stands and gives chase, hoping her face is managing to conceal her urgent need to get the laptop back. But Dan is dancing easily out of her way, the earlier Bloody Mary having kicked his hangover further down the road. He's perky and playful. Anna reaches, laughs, but she has no chance against Dan's height and long limbs. She grabs the towel around his waist and yanks it, whooping as it abandons him. Stark naked, he looks at her, gloriously unabashed. She lunges closer, but he steps back and swings the laptop behind his body, trying to manoeuvre her into an embrace. Anna sees it before it happens. The laptop in Dan's right arm is tracing a perfect arc towards the tall ugly vase on the console table by the front door. She is too far away to stop it. Time slows as the laptop connects with the vase and Anna closes her eyes against the whack, topple and smash. The vase disintegrates, time resumes, and they both stand guiltily in the ensuing silence.

'Well, in fairness that vase deserved to die.'

'Oh, Dan.'

Dan shrugs his shoulders, then begins to jive his naked body, his floppy penis slapping off one thigh, then the other. It always cracks Anna up.

'Stop, Dan!' she laughs. 'Careful!'

Dan's bare feet are surrounded by various-sized chunks and slivers of coloured glass. He tiptoes away from the debris.

'What's this?' Anna has spotted something else among the shards on the floor. 'Strange. This must have been in the vase.' She crouches down and picks up a plain key, no keyring attached. She puts it in the empty fruit bowl on the kitchen counter.

'Dan, you'd better message Mrs Cassidy and let her know. I've an awful feeling that the world's most hideous vase held a special place in the old woman's heart. You get dressed, I'll sweep up this mess.'

'Okay. Ta.' He turns to her, from halfway up the stairs. 'And then we'll go for a pub lunch?'

'Sure. Sounds good.'

Anna sweeps up the shards quickly and drops them into the kitchen bin. While Dan's moving around upstairs getting dressed, she grabs the laptop off the console table, shuts the browser tab and breathes out a sigh of relief. She's closing the laptop again just as Dan's shoes appear at the top of the stairs.

She should tell him about the lack of recent reviews. He has a right to know. He's halfway down the stairs now, whistling tunelessly to himself.

'Hey, Dan?'

'What, love?' He's smiling at her.

Anna swallows, pushing it all down. She'll not ruin their nice weekend.

'I'm starving.'

# NINE

THE FIESTA STOPS at the end of the brambly laneway.

'Alright, love. Your choice. Left or right.'

Anna cranes her neck forward, glancing down to the left, but the overgrown hedgerows obscure any view. She pictures the abandoned abattoir further along the road in that direction.

'Let's go right.'

They pass very little of interest on the road. A boarded-up primary school, then a fire-damaged house. To Anna, there's a whiff of tragedy about this place, an air of abandonment hanging over everything, as if the living have all moved on. Just like the Cassidy house, she thinks to herself. They pass a couple of gates with *Keep Out* and *Beware of Dog!* signs. And just when they begin to wonder if they should turn around, they spot a church steeple in the distance, and soon enough they're entering a compact village with a butcher, a newsagent, three pubs and a hairdresser. Dan pulls the car into a gravelled parking lot to the side of one of the pubs and is holding open the door of Slattery's Bar for Anna before she's even swung her legs out of the car.

'Jeez, Dan, you're keen!'

His hand reaches for the small of Anna's back to guide her into the bar, and she is shocked at the sudden urge she feels to turn around and collapse into him, bury her head in his shoulder and beg him not to get on the plane next week. Instead she fixes a smile on her face. It's not like Dan's got any choice in the matter.

Inside, Anna chooses a table for two by the window, a ceramic pot of violet-blossomed hydrangea on the deep sill.

'What'll it be, love?'

Anna glances towards the mahogany bar, where a middle-aged woman with short grey hair is restocking the salted nuts.

'The usual please. Soda water. With fresh lime if they have it...'

The woman has been glancing over circumspectly, no doubt trying to work out who they are. Anna doubts they'd have too many tourists passing through. She smiles at the thought of herself being a tourist. Over at the bar, Dan's Aussie accent seems to bounce off every wall in the place. A couple of old men at the far end of the bar look up from their newspapers, before quickly losing interest in the stranger in their local. The bar woman smiles, then starts on his pint of Guinness. Anna wiggles her bum on the thin cushion of the bench seat and reaches across for the menu on the neighbouring table. The walk to the quarry this morning seems to have given her an appetite. She's glad they got out for a spin and a break from that miserable house. She breathes out slowly, and puts her elbows on the table, resting her chin on her nested fingers so that she hopefully looks relaxed. Dan turns and carries their glasses across, winking at her as he places their drinks down. Anna raises her glass.

'Here's to you, Daniel Pell.' A lump comes to Anna's throat, but she pushes on. 'You're a good man, and I haven't said it much recently, but I do love you. Very much.' As Daniel's hand squeezes her leg under the table, Anna blinks back tears. 'I'm going to miss you.' This comes out as a whisper, Anna's voice on the point of breaking, and she has to look at her glass for a moment, to steady herself, before she raises her drink to his. Dan lifts his pint to clink Anna's glass, then they both take a sip in silence. When Anna looks at him, Dan is staring off to the middle distance, a furrow in his brow. He blinks himself back into the moment, noticing her observing him.

'I'm going to miss you heaps, too.'

His fingers wrap snugly around Anna's hands on the table, his thumb rubbing lightly along her wrist.

'Penny for your thoughts?'

He opens his mouth, a momentary pause, then withdraws his hand as he sits back in his chair.

'I was just thinking I could eat a horse. Shall we order?'

He has grabbed the menu and swivelled it around to face himself. Anna steals a moment to try and capture his face in her mind. He might be sitting only inches from her, but already Anna can sense he's begun to slip away from her, already caught up in the reality of moving back to his home country in a matter of days. Anna's been so self-absorbed recently, that she hasn't taken a minute to think of things from his perspective. Of course he can't fully be here. This chapter in his life is about to close. Anna looks at his fingers drumming the menu. She wants to grab his hand and chain herself to him, to never let him go. But a pair of sensible black shoes has shuffled into Anna's peripheral vision. She glances up to find the woman from behind the bar hovering with a pencil and pad.

'Now, folks. What can I get you?'

When their plates are clean, Dan excuses himself to pop to the Gents. Sensible shoes is back to clear the table.

'How was everything?'

'Lovely, thanks.'

The woman motions to the empty glasses. 'Another round of drinks?'

Anna thinks back to the fusty house. She's in absolutely no rush to get back. 'Sure, that would be great. Thanks.'

'No bother. I'll drop them down to you.' The woman has stacked their plates and is using Dan's scrunched up serviette to mop up some dribbles from Anna's glass off the table. 'So, just passing through?'

'Yeah. We're down from Dublin for the weekend. Staying in a house just up the road.'

'Very good.' The woman shifts her weight from one hip to the other. 'Of course we used to get a lot more visitors through here. But things have gone very quiet over the past year or so.' She frowns at the pot of hydrangeas, momentarily lost in thought. 'There was a woman up near the lake who used to rent out her place. Lovely Mrs Cassidy. But that obviously—'

'Oh, that's where we're staying. We're in Mrs Cassidy's while she stays up at my place in Dublin. We're doing a house swap with her for the …'

Anna's words trail off. A strange look is haunting the woman's face, an unsure smile which soon hardens into something far less kind as Anna's been speaking.

'I don't find that amusing. Old Mrs Cass—'

Dan has arrived back and is pulling his stool out noisily.

'Sorry, don't mind me.'

But the woman says nothing more. She glares at Anna a moment longer, barely concealed reproach in her eyes, before she turns on her heel.

'Did I miss something?'

Anna shrugs, clueless, as she watches the woman disappear behind the bar.

'You finish your drink. I'm going to nip across the road and buy some milk and ciggies. You want anything?'

'Hmm?'

Anna can't take her eyes off the bar woman. She's now at the far end of the bar, deep in conversation with the two old men, their newspapers abandoned. One of the men nods in Anna's direction, and when the woman turns, she merely casts Anna a sour look, before turning to resume her conversation. She'll be bringing them no more drinks. Anna's cheeks burn.

'I said, did you want anything? From the shop?' Dan is shoving his hands into his jacket sleeves, unaware of the frostiness that has descended.

'No, no, you're good. Sorry. I might just wait outside.'

Anna stands quietly, leaving her drink, and follows Dan out into the glare of the afternoon. While he jogs across to the shop, Anna walks slowly to the car, the memory of the woman's bitter expression trailing her like a bad smell. Her rudeness is going to needle Anna's thoughts all afternoon. Anna should go back in there right now, challenge her, ask her what the hell she did wrong. But she won't. She's never been one to make a fuss.

In the privacy of the car, Anna wishes they could just drive back to Skerries right now. She allows herself to groan aloud at the thought of another night in Mrs Cassidy's fusty old hovel. Then she remembers that Dan is planning to cook them a roast dinner tonight. That'll be nice. She'll focus on that. Anna closes her eyes and forces her body to relax against the rigid passenger seat, reminding herself that they'll be home this time tomorrow. One more night in the stranger's bed won't kill her.

# TEN

THE OLD MAN BEHIND THE SHOP COUNTER has ears the size of an Indian elephant. He's shrunken with age and his faded grey waistcoat hangs loose on him as he moves stiffly to find the pack of John Player Blues. The cigarettes are at shoulder height, and Dan is glad that the old codger doesn't need to climb up on a stool to retrieve them.

'Now,' he says, sliding the pack across the counter. 'Anything else?'

'Yeah, could I get a pouch of rolling tobacco. And some rolling papers too, mate. Rizzlas, if you have them.'

A rheumy eye flickers up to meet Dan's for a moment, before the man turns stiffly once more to the shelves. Dan suppresses a smile. The old bloke places the items on the counter.

'Australia. Is it?'

'Sure is. And I thought I was blending in.'

The shopkeeper smiles at this, then starts totting up the items on a large calculator. 'We don't get too many from your part of the world, or from anywhere else, for that matter. Of course, we used to get the odd tourist...'

'Yeah...?' Dan's looking forward to getting back to the house. He really enjoyed his pint. But now he's ready for a nice fat joint and a glass or two of red on the sofa.

'There was a woman just up the road,' the shopkeeper continues. 'Used to rent out her house to the tourists, like yourself. And they'd swing by here. Twas good for business, so it was. Dried up now though.'

'Is that right?'

The screen on the calculator seems to be fading to grey. The man picks it up and gives it a practised smack on the counter before resuming.

'Course that ended. Terrible business altogether. No more visitors to our wee backwater now.'

Dan taps his thigh with his credit card, remembering the antsy scowl on Anna's face as she came out of the pub. He knows what will cheer her up.

'Actually, mate, I'll grab a Lotto ticket too.'

The old man shuffles down the length of the counter and pushes a few buttons on the console.

'Six million tonight,' he shouts across to Dan. 'But sure you can't take it with you when you die.'

Dan grunts his agreement as the shopkeeper shuffles back with the ticket in his arthritic hand.

'I've yet to see a hearse with a tow bar. Am I right?' He slides the lottery ticket towards Dan. 'Lorna Cassidy.' He turns his calculator with its grand total around to face Dan. 'If you have cash it would be easier.'

Dan frowns at the counter, repeating in his mind the name he's just heard. He looks into the old fella's watery grey eyes.

'That name you just mentioned. Lorna Cassidy?'

'That was her name. The woman that owned the house for the tourists. Died last year, so she did.'

For a moment the shopkeeper observes Dan warily, as if the tall Australian on the other side of his counter is intellectually impaired. Then he pulls Dan's notes and coins towards himself, dropping the coins into the various compartments of the cash register drawer.

'God rest her soul. No-one left now, apart from that gobshite of a son. Lorna never got on with him. Kicked him out after the father died. He was her stepson, you see. A surly fecker.'

The shopkeeper pushes the drawer of the till closed with a satisfying rattle and leans his folded arms on the counter. 'A surly fecker, indeed. A loner. Even the other lads in the abattoir kept their distance when he worked there.' The old man leans in a fraction closer and lowers his voice. 'It was said he enjoyed the butchering a bit too much. Sick bastard. Liked to torture the poor animals.' He shakes his head at the thought and suddenly seems to regret sharing so much with the stranger in his shop. He clears his throat and steps back. 'Anyway...' He pauses when he notices Dan's expression.

'This Lorna Cassidy...' Dan's voice is low, tentative. 'Who looks after her house now?'

The man looks at him blankly for a moment. 'No-one. There's only the stepson left. And you wouldn't want to be crossing paths with him.'

Two young girls, twin sisters with inky black hair and shockingly pale skin, slip silently in front of Dan and now stand patiently at the counter. Both stare vacantly at the big tubs of sweets on the buckling shelf. The old man takes down the plastic tub of jelly snakes and sets it on the counter, nothing spoken.

At the doorway Dan stops. 'And what's his name, this stepson?'

The shopkeeper is struggling to unscrew the lid from the jelly snakes. He frowns across at the Australian. 'Well, since the accident, he'd be known as Hopalong. Although you wouldn't want to be calling him that to his face, so you wouldn't.' The lid comes off the jar and clatters to the floor. The man mumbles a curse to himself and bends with difficulty, then stands up, red-faced. 'He's queer in the head, either way.' He counts out the snakes onto the counter with his grubby fingers. 'Now girls, did ye want them in separate bags…?'

Outside, Dan stops by the green post box near the entrance to the shop. His throat is dry and there's an itchy heat in his scalp. He just needs a moment. From his semi-hidden position he can see across the road to the pub car park. Anna is resting her eyes in the car. Dan holds his position, his gaze momentarily drawn to the pavement, as if the bird shit and chewing gum hold the answers to his confusion. A few dead leaves swirl near his ankles, buffeted by the westerly wind which seems to be strengthening steadily.

Maybe the old man was confused. What else could it be? After all, Dan had been back-and-forthing with Lorna Cassidy over the past few days when he did the booking. He thinks of her smiling profile picture on the house swap website. Each message had been signed off with 'LC'. Hadn't it? Dan gnaws at the flaking skin on his bottom lip, doubt creeping into his memory now.

Only a couple of hours ago, when Anna had gone upstairs to do her hair, Dan had bashed out a snarky message to Lorna Cassidy via the house swap website. After all, Anna had insisted he message their host about them breaking the fugly vase, its glass shards now in the belly of the kitchen bin.

But Dan hadn't exactly stuck to script. Sticking to script, as per Anna's instructions, would have involved simply telling Mrs Cassidy about the broken vase, and asking if the two cats were okay. No, he'd been a bit more … *blunt*. He hadn't realised until he'd started typing just how pissed off he'd been with the whole experience. He hadn't been rude — not exactly — but had simply wanted to give this Mrs Cassidy some timely feedback, an opportunity to make things right. Dan had always hated keyboard warriors, those weaklings who blasted off passive-aggressive missives from their bedrooms, leaving one-star ratings and nasty reviews. Always better to allow people to step up, to fix issues in the moment, that was his approach.

A niggling disquiet rolls through Dan's gut. Maybe he'd been a little *too* blunt. He'd said the place was dank and unwelcoming, that the air was stale and the towels were musty. He'd devoted an entire paragraph to how unacceptable the approach to the house was, the laneway overgrown and his girlfriend nearly losing an eye due to those lethal brambles. He cringes now.

*Lethal brambles.*

And he'd ranted about the dead plants and the layer of dust and the fact there'd been no easy way to contact the host cos she'd not bothered to take her bloody mobile phone with her. Dan winces further. He'd also threatened to leave a one-star rating and a less than stellar review unless she could make things right. Christ. He *was* that keyboard warrior.

Dan sucks in through his clenched teeth, then closes his eyes in an attempt to block everything out. He needs to think for a moment. But the shopkeeper's words replay in his head.

*Died last year....*

So, who the hell had Dan just blasted off a snarky message to — and more to the point — who was staying in Anna's cottage in Skerries?

A familiar horn toots twice. Dan raises a hand.

'Sorry, love. Coming!' He jogs across the empty road to the car. 'Just had a cramp in my leg.'

'Everything alright? You look a bit distracted.'

He should tell her. See what she thinks of the old man's theory. Maybe they'll both laugh at the craziness of it. Dan climbs into the car. No, there's no point worrying her over something which is very likely a big steaming pile of crap. The old man in the shop might be suffering from dementia. But Dan's hunch is that the guy is just one of those mischievous characters who enjoys taking the piss out of hapless tourists who wander in.

That's all it is, Dan convinces himself. He glances across at Anna and notices her faraway stare. He'll say nothing. There's obviously something already bothering her.

'No, all good, love.'

He leans across to kiss Anna's neck, rubbing his stubble across her skin until she laughs and twists her body away from his. Anything to stop her looking too closely at his face.

# June

# ELEVEN

ANNA PUSHED CLOSED THE SKYLIGHT above her bed and made a mental note to clean the seagull shit off the glass at some stage. She kicked some stray shoes out of the way, no time to tidy the mess now, then glanced at her watch.

'Ger, remind me which train we're taking?' Anna shouted across the upstairs landing.

The other bedroom door stood slightly ajar, dry-cleaning hooked on the doorknob, summer frocks and a feather boa draped over the top. Ger was hopping around, trying to cram her foot into a new suede ankle boot.

'It's in half an hour, hon. If we leave here in five minutes we'll be grand.'

'Cool.'

Lorcan, Ger's older brother, was back from New York on a flying visit with his wife and two young kids, and Anna and Ger were heading into Dublin city centre to meet them all. It had been a good seven years since Anna last saw Lorcan, at his wedding, and now as she applied some lippy in her bedroom mirror, she smiled at the memory of them snogging at a party one summer when they were both awkward teens. A lifetime ago. Ger's family had become even more important to Anna in the three years since her own parents had passed away: six months apart, first her Mum from cancer, then her Dad from heart disease. Alice and Brendan, childhood sweethearts, who'd been told they'd never have children, only for Alice to experience a miraculous conception at age forty-two. Leaning over to her nightstand, Anna adjusted the small silver framed picture of her parents on their wedding day, then stood back and sighed. At least she had Ger and her folks. They were as good as family, and Anna would never take them for granted. She grabbed the two brightly wrapped presents she'd bought for Lorcan's two kids, Harper and Roman, and squirrelled them into her bag.

As she hurried down the stairs, she took a critical look at herself in the hall mirror, remembering how effortlessly chic Lorcan's wife, Michelle, was. She stood for a moment, considering running back upstairs to change, when a hard knock on the front door made her jump. Dan was standing on the doorstep in his hi-vis jacket, the knees of his jeans covered in plaster dust.

'Oh, hello. I wasn't expecting you.'

He leaned in for a kiss, his warm woody scent stirring something inside Anna.

'I was doing a job up the road and was just on my way back to the flat when I thought I might swing by and surprise my woman.'

Anna stepped back to let him in. 'Ah, you're sweet. But listen, you can only come in for a minute. We're about to head into the city to meet Ger's brother.'

Ger's voice bounced down from upstairs. 'Hiya, Danny Boy.'

'Hey, Ger Bear.'

Anna lead Dan to the kitchen, his fingers playing gently on her hip as he followed. When they reached the dining table he spun her around, dropped his backpack onto the slate tiled floor, then pulling her in for a long kiss. He tasted of coffee, cigarettes and longing. He pushed against her. *So that's why he's here*, she thought to herself. She laughed and lightly shoved him back.

'Down boy! I gotta finish getting ready.' Anna darted through to the downstairs loo, beyond the kitchen, shouting over her shoulder. 'Stick the kettle on if you want a cuppa? But you'll need to be quick, Dan. Sorry to rush you. It's Lorcan's only weekend in Dublin, then they're off to Edinburgh, and—'

'Lorcan?'

Anna dabbed some perfume onto her wrists and neck, then checked her teeth in the mirror over the basin. 'Ger's brother. I just told you. Anyway…'

She could hear the suck and rattle of the fridge door opening, followed by a familiar clink. When she emerged from the loo, Dan had his arse parked against the kitchen table, an open bottle of Heineken angled to his lips. As she approached him, her eyebrow raised, he held out a second bottle towards her, already open.

'Time for a quick one?'

The innuendo was not subtle. Anna took a long swig of the cool beer and stood with her legs straddling his right thigh.

'You're a bad influence, Daniel Pell.'

'You're not so innocent yourself, Anna Moriarty.' He pulled her towards him. His voice was quietened to a hot, insistent whisper in Anna's ear, his bottom lip brushing her earlobe. He had raised a fingertip to her face and now gently traced it down her cheek and neck. Above them, Ger's bedroom door creaked, followed by footsteps bounding down the stairs. Anna set her bottle down and took a step back, as Ger swept into the kitchen, her face flushed, her eyes bright. She ruffled Dan's hair as she passed the table, before spotting the second open beer bottle near Anna.

'Jeez, you're a bad influence, Daniel Pell.'

'That's what I said!' agreed Anna.

Ger glanced at the wall clock near the window, shrugged on her jacket and nodded to Anna.

'We should make a move. Dan, I'd invite you to join us, but it's a strictly no weirdos lunch.'

Dan laughed. 'No offence taken, I'm sure.' He raised the bottle to his lips again, but kept his eyes fixed on Anna, a playful hunger for her barely concealed. Ger leaned outside to tip the dregs of a pint glass of water into a pot of sweet peas on the back patio, then pulled on the sliding glass door. It slammed shut with an unequivocal thud, causing Anna to jump.

'Sorry guys. I'll take my fingers off one of these days. Anna, shall we?'

Dan had taken hold of Anna's wrist, the pad of his thumb caressing her pulse point.

'Actually, Ger, would you mind if Anna followed you in on the next train?' His eyes were still locked on Anna's. Her face flushed.

'Er, I guess? Anna, you're still coming, right?'

Anna looked sheepishly up at her friend. Ger was doing her best not to look peeved, but Anna could see the hint of disappointment in her eyes. No, Anna would stick to their agreed plan.

'No, Dan, I can't. I should—'

'Come on, Banana. Just catch the next train. Ger doesn't mind, do you, Ger?'

A flit of irritation passed over Ger's face, and she looked directly at Anna when she spoke.

'That's fine. But Anna, don't let me down. Lorcan's really looking forward to seeing you after all these years. We planned this ages ago.' She jiggled her bag to close its zip, then glanced back from the door. 'See you in a bit, yeah?'

'I promise, Ger. I'll be there.'

And with that, Ger was gone, the front door tugged firmly closed behind her.

Anna groaned and leaned her forehead against Dan's shoulder. 'Dan, did I ever tell you you're a bad influence?'

His hands had travelled down her back and now cupped her arse, guiding her firmly closer.

'Well, if you're going to be a little late, we might as well make it worth your while…'

Anna's jacket tumbled to the kitchen floor as Dan began to slowly unbutton her blouse. His mouth was on her mouth, then her neck, and breasts, her skin tingling. He explored her with a ravenous energy, clumsy fingers pulling at her bra clasp, then tugging at the button on her jeans. Something base and animal lurked in his eyes, distant and determined, a primal urge as he spun Anna around and pushed her body, face down, across the table. His muscular thighs forced her legs apart and she gasped as he entered her, no time wasted. She instantly lost herself, fully in her body, as the rhythmic pleasure built steadily between them.

Ger's two rescue cats watched on from the other side of the sliding glass door. Anna turned her head as Dan continued, his thrusts non-negotiable. He stepped closer, moving even deeper inside her. Dan has always been a considerate lover, his lovemaking with Anna slow and tentative, always sure to never leave her behind. But now he was like a man possessed. His wide hands tugged Anna's hips, forcing her to grip the edge of the table with her fingers. And now he was faster, his moves rougher, as he grunted and edged his way closer to his reward. Anna would allow him this today. Being here, beneath his bulk, feeling the power of desire she held over him, this was enough for her today.

Her cheek was pressed against the tabletop. In front of her was the framed photograph. The picture Dan took of Ger and Anna in the cafe the day he met them both. The two smiling faces watched Anna as Dan approached his climax. Anna closed her eyes as his thrusts subsided. He collapsed on her, his heavy chest heaving against her back, his breathing loud and laboured in her ear.

'What was that?' His words were hot on the side of her face. 'That noise.'

Anna opened her eyes. The picture was gone. The frame must have fallen to the slate tiled kitchen floor below. Dan kissed the nape of her neck, then pushed himself up and away. He pulled up his jocks and trousers, slid open the door and shooed the cats away, then took a swig from his beer bottle. Anna remained there, laid across the table for a moment, exposed and vulnerable, waiting for her own breathing to return to normal.

She pushed her hot face away from the table and leaned over the side, craning her neck so she could look down at the broken picture frame on the hard floor below. The photograph of herself and Ger was perfectly intact, but the glass had split into two pieces now, a sinewy seam running up between their faces. A crack in the surface of a frozen lake, a warning to Anna to watch her step.

# October

# TWELVE

DAN TAKES OUT THE BOTTLE OF CHAMPAGNE from his weekend bag and places it on the bottom shelf of the fridge. He stands motionless at the fridge door for a moment in the weak yellow patch of light. His thoughts are fuggy from the joint he just smoked. It's mid-afternoon and Anna is down at the lake, but he needs to decide before she gets back. Cold air trails out from the fridge and down to his feet.

He grabs the bottle and slips it back into his bag on the dining table, then stares blankly at it. He glances out the kitchen window to make sure Anna's not about to walk in on him, then grips the countertop and exhales in frustration at his indecision.

On Thursday morning he'll be buckled into his seat on the first of two flights which will take him back to Australia. Does he really want Anna buckled into the seat beside him?

In his bag is an envelope containing a ticket in her name. A one-month return trip that will give Anna enough time to see if she could imagine a future with him in Australia. He's spoken to his sister in Tamarama, and her spare room is ready and waiting for them. For the past few weeks the planned surprise has brought a much-needed smile to Dan's lips, and he's nearly let it slip a few times. But now the time is fast approaching when he has to ask Anna. He can't realistically delay it any longer. She'll need time to arrange things, get herself into the right head space.

Dan rubs his hand down his face. He thought he knew what he wanted, but these past few months have worn him down. He takes a long slug of red wine straight from the bottle. Anna's been getting worse lately, and he's begun to wonder if she'll ever bounce back. This is more than grieving for a lost friend. Anna's drifted into obsessive compulsive territory. He's heard her, on the nights he stays over, secretively double-checking the snib on the patio door, and triple-checking the locks on the front door. She stands at the front room curtain, lost in her thoughts, convinced the house is being watched. The fact that she's doing it discreetly means she's aware it's not healthy. And then there's the nightmares, the wary glances over her shoulder, the incessant scrolling of the news feed, and her manic theory about some guy in a white van.

Dan steps back from the sink and forces a slow twist into his spine, promising himself he won't end up sleeping on the lumpy sofa again tonight. He takes out the sealed envelope from the bottom of his bag and stares at it blankly. If he does invite her back with him, which version of Anna would he be bringing to Australia?

When he conjures up an image of Anna these days, it's of a woman ploughing down the village streets of Skerries with a stack of *Missing Person* posters tucked tight under her arm. Her jaw set, her balled fists rammed into her jacket pockets, an invisible aura of black anger scaring away friends and neighbours. He observed her like this in reality once, when she didn't notice him watching from the street corner. And he'd wanted nothing more at the time than to take her in his arms and hold her tight, repeating in whispers to *let Ger go*, to *live again*. And in that fantasy, he would hold down her flailing limbs, and ignore her feral spitting, until her anger would break and finally bring hot tears in gulped shudders. But Dan has said nothing more than cliches in her ear these past three months, and now he wonders if he's missed his opportunity to say what he truly believes. He feels worse than useless most of the time, a mute bystander watching on as his woman slips further away from her true self, a raging stranger taking her place.

As he takes another swig of wine, an image comes to mind of Sergeant Rooney and his harried colleagues. Dan's first impressions of the browbeaten cop hadn't been great. On the Saturday morning back in July when Anna had dragged Dan to the copshop to report Ger missing, Joe Rooney had eyed Dan like he was Ireland's most wanted. But now Dan feels a certain comradeship with the man, both of them having been on the receiving end of Anna's grim determination.

Dan fingers the neck of the champagne bottle looking up at him from the bag. Maybe Anna will surprise him. Maybe the original version of Anna will make an appearance this evening when he asks her. The version he first met on that sunny April afternoon at the markets in Dublin city centre. The version who was sassy and funny, passionate and easy-going. Maybe he just needs to have faith that that girl's still in there somewhere.

He grabs the Bollinger from his bag once more, and hides it towards the back of the fridge. He won't give up on her yet. He owes her. Over on the dining table, a message pings on the laptop. Dan pulls out a dining chair and taps the laptop awake.

*Message from LC*

He laughs quietly to himself as he drags his finger across the touchpad, thinking back to the crazy old shopkeeper and his dark sense of humour.

*Lorna Cassidy… Died last year.*

Yeah, right, mate.

Dan clicks on the message and leans in towards the laptop. He sits back and frowns at the screen, scrolling up and down the body of the message, but it's completely blank. Then he sees it. There's an attachment. He double-clicks it and a full-screen video pops up. A moment passes before Dan understands what he's watching. Then his bowels twist.

Ger's two cats, Nip and Tuck, are outside on the patio at Anna's place, looking in towards the camera with wide-eyed fear. The camera pans down to show two bowls of cat food on the slate-tiled kitchen floor, just inside the sliding door. Out of shot, a hand has taken the handle of the door and is now slamming it closed, the door banging against the frame, then bouncing in its track. Dan's throat is dry. He watches as the door slides open again, and this time Dan can hear the bag of cat kibble being shaken, something Anna does to entice the cats in at night. Nip, the braver of the rescue cats, puts her front paw tentatively forward, then hesitates. She's smart, but she's hungry. The door slams shut again, with more than enough force to decapitate a cat. The video ends.

A blue vein pulses along the back of Dan's hand, and a sheen of cold sweat covers his forehead. He swallows, as reality hits him. The shopkeeper wasn't lying. Lorna Cassidy is dead. And her sicko stepson must be staying in Anna's house, after all. Dan closes the laptop slowly, a slight tremor in his hand. This can't be happening.

*And all because of a broken vase and a stroppy message?*

He stands and paces behind the sofa.

'Fuck!'

Anna's going to murder him.

'Fuck. Fuck. Fuck.'

If anything was to happen to those two cats… His thoughts begin to scramble for attention as he glances at his watch. He could leave Anna a note, make up some bullshit excuse and jump in the car right now. Within two hours, if he floors it, he could be dragging the guy out by the scruff of the neck and giving him a good thumping. He rubs the short hair on the back of his scalp. No, he can't just abandon Anna here on her own for the night.

*Think, Dan!*

Or he could phone Anna's neighbour, the nosy woman with the big tits. Get her to swing by the house. Juliette, that's her name. But what the hell would he say?

*Some dead woman's weirdo stepson is staying in Anna's house and has threatened the cats?*

He scoffs the idea away. No, better to say nothing to Juliette. She'd only call up Anna in a tizz and then Anna will have a full-blown meltdown.

Dan's limbs are fizzy as he heads out the front door. His initial shock at the video is now morphing into something else, a hot fury racing through his veins. His fingers have curled into fists and he desperately wants to punch something. But Anna will be on her way back. He needs to calm himself before she sees him.

He kicks at some loose gravel with the toe of his boot.

*Typical.*

Trust Dan to arrange a house swap with someone who's mad as a cut snake.

Overhead, there's the first of a series of grumbles, a dry fizz of electricity in the air. The wind has picked up and a branch taps against an upstairs window.

The old shopkeeper's words from earlier push into Dan's mind:

*Sick bastard...Liked to torture the animals*

Dan looks down to the gravel where his boot has scuffed the surface of the driveway, a few parallel shallow troughs now gouged at his foot. It reminds him of the concealed photograph he found last night in the study at the end of the corridor, a woman's face scored by something sharp and deliberate. No doubt the work of a resentful stepson. He rubs a hand down his face, then remembers the stepson's nickname.

*Hopalong.*

Above him, the pregnant clouds are on the point of bursting. Dan forces himself to breathe slowly, his jaw tense, his shoulders rigid. He's going to have to teach this Hopalong kid a lesson. No-one threatens Daniel Pell.

The overhead branch is banging against the bedroom window frame more insistently now. But it's not the branch that Dan hears. It's the violent slam of the patio door in Anna's kitchen. And when he closes his eyes against the noise, all he can see is the total fear in the eyes of those two bewildered cats.

Dan turns around to face the stranger's house, his mind whirring, the taste for vengeance on his lips. First thing in the morning, he'll use the crappy weather as an excuse for himself and Anna to head home a few hours early. And when they arrive at Anna's house, he'll ask her to wait in the car for a few minutes. Then he'll walk in on this Hopalong freak and drag him out into the back garden, where he'll take slow pleasure in knocking ten shades of shite out of the little weirdo, Dan's months of boxing training at the gym finally able to be put to some use.

Dan cricks his neck and cracks his knuckles, content to have a plan in place. But in the meantime, he's itching for a little bit of instant gratification. He chews his bottom lip as he looks at the front of the house.

*So this Hopalong character wants to play games?*

The sense of impotence leaves him as he walks purposefully up the steps. Before he closes the front door, he glances back down the path to check that Anna isn't about to return. He just needs enough time to cause the weirdo a little pain of his own.

# THIRTEEN

ANNA STUFFS HER SOCKS INTO HER TRAINERS and places them on a flat rock by the water's edge. Above her, the thick welt of cloud has darkened into deep layers of pewter. She rolls up the bottom of her jeans and steps gingerly across the muddy bank into the chill water of the lake. Mud oozes up between her toes and she stands still in the shin-deep water, blinking away a streak of tears the cutting wind has drawn from her eyes. Over on the far side of the lake a pair of swans nestle in a barely protected feeder creek. Anna shuffles further from the shoreline, her pale feet now a blur in the disturbed sediment.

She closes her eyes and works her toes deeper into the mud, the chill of the water momentarily dampening her dark thoughts. She'd forgotten how grounding water can be, the weekend swims at the North Strand having stopped when Ger vanished. Maybe Anna should have kept up those Saturday swims on her own for the sake of her sanity. The water has soaked the bottom of her turn-ups, but she doesn't care. If only it could drain away the guilt and anxiety, all the darkness, from her body, and bury it under the layers of silt and rotting weeds, to leave her in peace.

It's three months today. Three whole months and nothing to show for it. Anna closes her eyes and puffs out her cheeks as she remembers this morning's phone call with Joe Rooney at the quarry. He'd been a total prick, so quick to dismiss Anna's theory about a link to the latest abduction attempt. She shakes her head at his offhandedness and reminds herself that she can't rely on the cops anymore. They've had more than enough opportunities to get a handle on this case and all they've done is waste precious time. She'll just have to do Rooney's job for him.

Again, Anna is aware of an insistent tension which has been slowly creeping up her spine all morning. She'd blamed it on the soft mattress she slept on last night. But standing here alone in the lake water, she can finally admit that it's because she's absolutely terrified she's about to permanently unravel. As she inhales a long cool breath, she decides there and then that when Dan walks out the front door for the airport on Thursday morning, she will allow herself twenty-four hours, and not one minute more. Twenty-four hours when she will let the waves of despair and loss crash over her and batter her into submission. Twenty-four hours to crumble and wallow and cry herself dry. A whole day to snivel and let the dark thoughts run rampant within, alone again, with no witnesses to shame her out of her black mood. And when those twenty-four hours are up, Anna will dust herself off and drag herself to her feet, shoving all the pain deep down to a place she'll padlock shut. She'll keep her anger close at hand, though, for that will drive her forward, propel her through the winter months ahead and fuel her to leave no stone unturned in her search for Ger.

From behind her comes the creak and rustle of trees, the disgruntled cries of ruffled birds. She lets her vision drift over the choppy lake water. Something's up with Dan. He's been cagey all weekend, like he knows something Anna doesn't. She stares at the creek in the distance as she lets her thoughts percolate. And it hits her, how totally self-absorbed she's been these past three months. Dan's been struggling too, but it's as if Anna claimed the monopoly on grief. When was the last time she bothered to ask him how *he* was doing? Ger had been like a sister to him and it shames Anna now to admit she's left him zero room to express his own pain. The man deserves a proper send-off. Until he walks out of her life on Thursday morning, she'll give him her undivided attention. She'll say nothing negative about the crappy house. She'll not nag him to check up on Mrs Cassidy or the two cats. She'll trust him to be the capable adult he is. No more wasted time on phone calls to Sergeant Rooney. No scrolling the news first thing in the morning. Anna will be her former fun-loving self until Dan leaves for the airport. She'll send him off with a smile and some happy memories of his time in Ireland. Even if the effort kills her on the inside.

A whip of damp hair has plastered itself across Anna's eyes. She turns to face the wind to free it, but as she does so she spots movement. Further along the shoreline, something has come to a sudden stop. A figure holds itself still in a tangled copse of spruce trees near the water's edge. It's not an animal. It's not a swaying branch. It's a person. Anna swallows. She stands rigid, cornered prey, her heart racing. This is private property. She stares, unblinking, but the wind blurs her vision. For once she wants it to be simple paranoia. But her mind is not playing tricks, not this time. The outline doesn't belong to Dan. It's a stranger, a man, watching her from the shadows.

All of a sudden, the figure, furtive in the gloom, starts to move steadily away. Anna splashes back to the muddy bank, stumbling into her shoes and shoving her socks into her jacket pocket. She looks once more over in his direction, but she's lost him, unable to see beyond the nearest thicket of trees.

Ahead of her lies the path back to the safety of the house. Anna starts quickly along it. There's no point calling Dan's name. Her shouts will be snatched by the wind. She'll run home and tell him. Her breath is heavy and her stomach churns, yet her feet come to a sudden stop. She turns her head and peers across the murky undergrowth, only stumps and rotting branches in the direction of the stranger. And once more she glances back up the path in the direction of the house, where Dan will be waiting for her, safe and warm. And in that instant, a realisation grips Anna and shakes her, surprising her and frightening her in equal measure. She needs to stop running. She is so very tired, tired of constantly looking over her shoulder, tired of fleeing knife-wielding monsters in her dreams. She's done with being passive and she's fed up waiting for other people to come to her rescue.

Anna sweeps a wild tangle of hair back from her face, then clambers across a mossy boulder into the shadows. And she wonders what in God's name she's doing.

# FOURTEEN

ANNA COMES TO AN ABRUPT STOP at the edge of a clearing, her hands on her hips, the metallic taste of blood on her gums. She sucks in jagged breaths. Her ankles, exposed below her rolled-up jeans, are covered in cuts and nettle stings. Seed pods cling to her jacket. She glances back into the dank forest behind. The towering trees are devoid of bird life, not even a stir of wind up here. But there is a distant howl, ghostly, in the near distance. She wipes the hair back from her forehead and slowly surveys the clearing in front of her. The man is nowhere to be seen. She curses to herself and hobbles forward, then kicks off her left shoe, before pouring out a sepia dribble of stagnant water. When she touches her stinging cheek she finds blood on her fingertip.

*Damn it, Anna!*

She straightens up, annoyed at her recklessness, and stuffs her bare foot back into the wet shoe. She has no clue how much ground she's covered in the past few minutes of scrambling through the undergrowth — possibly a kilometre, maybe more — but whoever was watching her back at the lake has vanished without a trace.

On the far edge of the clearing, beyond some straggly bushes, sits a wooden shack. Anna moves cautiously towards it. The windows on either side of the door are heavy with grime, and from here Anna can see a padlock on the door. She moves closer still, her footsteps tentative. The exterior walls are mottled with moss and mildew, and in places have rust-coloured streaks. Off to the left, a tractor tyre lies on its side. To the right, is the shell of a burnt-out car, its wheel hubs sitting on concrete blocks. She glances behind her and pauses for a moment. Apart from the grumbling sky there is not even the faintest buzz of an insect to kill the silence.

By her watch it's already gone four o'clock. Anna shakes her head, feeling suddenly foolish at chasing a stranger through the woods. The man she spotted was probably just some local farmer who had ventured onto the Cassidy property. Anna exhales through her cheeks. Dan will be wondering where she's got to. She'll head back, tell him she went for a bit of a ramble, then have a nice soak in the bath. Maybe even invite him to join her.

Above her, the darkening sky hangs heavy and low, barely able to suspend the imminent deluge. Anna sidles up to the shack and turns her back to it, surveying the shadowy wall of forest once more. She didn't think this through. Clambering back through those bushes and briars again does not appeal. She tuts to herself and finds her fingers raised once more to the cut on her cheek. She can only hope that whatever tugged at the skin doesn't leave a scar. As her eyes scan the ground over to her left, she notices a small path through the grass, barely visible, but present nonetheless. It seems to veer off in a direction which might just take her back towards the Cassidy house. She kicks off both shoes so she can pull on the socks which she had stuffed into her jacket pocket. Then she wedges her feet back into her shoes and laces them up. As she straightens, her hip knocks the padlock on the door behind her, and she turns to inspect it, giving it a firm tug before letting it knock back against the wood, the echo like a gunshot.

She sidles up to one of the grimy windows and uses the cuff of her denim jacket to wipe away some of the gunk from the pane. She should mind her own business, but what harm has a bit of curiosity ever done?

With her forehead resting against the glass, she cups her hands around her eyes. Someone has stayed here at some stage. It seems to be a single room, with a bare mattress in the corner of the filthy floor. At the other end sits a folding table with a small camping stove, a plastic tub and a couple of tin mugs. Not exactly luxury. Her eyes rove, her breath leaving little hot clouds of vapour on the dirty glass. On the opposite wall from her is another window, also filthy, looking out the back of the shack to where the forest restarts. As Anna's eyes continue to explore, her gaze is drawn upward. A menace of knives and cutting implements of every size dangle from iron hooks on the inside walls. And now she sees animal pelts stretched tight over frames, butchered rabbits and foxes and god-knows-what. Closer still, just below the window she is peering through, is a small table jammed with clusters of bottles and jars. Anna struggles to make out the detail of the contents through the dirty window. But memories of chemistry lab at school spring to mind. She can almost smell the formaldehyde from all those years ago in the science lab, bulls' eyes and frogs, after clumsy dissection by young, unsure hands.

Anna's not a superstitious person, but she's aware a cold shiver has just run down the length of her spine. The place is beyond creepy, a sharp scent of evil in the air.

She turns to leave, her eyes on the thin winding path, when she hesitates. Something is tugging at the back of her consciousness, calling her back to the window for something she missed. She leans back in, cupping her hands tighter against the glass. Among all the detritus, near the old mattress, is something black and sleek and totally out of place. A tripod for a camera.

*Huh… why on earth would—*

Anna freezes. Someone just moved beyond the far window. She jumps back from her own window, as if scalded, her breath held as she walks blindly backwards. She keeps her eyes locked on the front of the house, her feet tripping over crushed beer cans and smashed bottles. Her ankle clips a concrete block and Anna falls backwards, landing with a dull thud, her back whacking the hard earth. She is instantly winded.

'You shouldn't be here.'

Anna scrambles back on her elbows, her eyes wide, searching for the owner of the voice. A scruffy man in his sixties has appeared at the corner of the shack. He is sharpening a stick with a blade, studying her. She knows this old man, his unruly head of thick white hair. She recognises his tatty suit, the cold stare, the paring knife. They passed him yesterday. He lives in the caravan by the overgrown laneway. Anna lies immobile, struggling to gulp air back into her winded lungs. Her heart races as he moves closer, splinters of wood sparking from the stick he's paring. Her throat is dry and tight.

'Please... I didn't mean—'

'No, you shouldn't be here,' he repeats in a low monotone, glancing over his shoulder to check they're alone. 'Hopalong might come back.' The old man moves his blade deftly to his throat, fixing Anna with a feral stare as he advances closer. 'He likes to cut and slice.'

Anna tries to edge away, but a shard of broken bottle under her back is about to pierce her skin. The old man flicks the blade, mimicking a slick slice across his jugular, his weathered face grotesque in its shameless lunacy.

'Please... I'm sorry. I—'

Anna hears her own gulping sobs, a dying fish in its final moments. For a fleeting moment she imagines how she'll look laid out in the morgue, tear-streaked paths through the grime on her bloodied cheeks, the terror of her last moments etched in her face.

'Makes them scream, so he does.' The old man glances back towards the shack again, a flash of uncertainty on his face. 'Likes them pretty.' His eyes are back on Anna now. He leans in, close enough for his knife to enter her. Anna holds her breath.

*This is it.*

She tries to shut her eyes, to block out this horror, but the old stranger's bloodshot eyes are locked on hers and Anna has no choice but to lie there, paralysed by the fear of what's coming.

'Not right.' The old man has raised his index finger to his temple and now swivels his hand. 'Not right in the head, at all.'

A fleck of spittle escapes the man's mouth and lands on Anna's face, jolting her as much as if it were a slap. Above them, the sky cracks in a blinding flash. The man stands, his face turned to the heavens. Anna seizes the moment. She flips herself onto her hands, stays low and scrambles, not daring to look back yet. She straightens and sprints, reaching the grass path in seconds, trees and shadows blurring in her vision.

The acid threat of bile arises in her stomach, but Anna forces it back down. Around her, the first fat drops of rain pepper the ground. She stops and turns, her chest burning, to confirm he's not in pursuit. In the distance, she can see him, still near the front of the shack. His arms are extended, a demented Jesus on the cross, the wickedness on his face raised to the heavens.

Another flash of lightning momentarily blinds the landscape. Anna turns and runs, already soaked to the skin, the old man's deranged expression burned into her retinas.

# FIFTEEN

'DAN?'

Anna slams the front door and slumps against it. Her breath is heavy in the silence. Her vision struggles in the dim light of the room.

'Dan?'

Behind her back, her hand fumbles, fingers groping for the snib, until the small lock clicks into place. Her body is completely drenched and water pools on the doormat beneath her feet. She wrings out a fistful of hair as another crack of lightning flares outside. A temper of thunder rolls across the house a moment later.

'Dan?'

She shirks off her saturated jacket to the floor and kicks off her soaked shoes.

Dan!'

*Where the hell is he?*

She pads across the room in her bare feet. The car is still parked out front, so he can't be far. She looks to the staircase. He must be having a nap, tired after his comatose night on the sofa. She hurries up to the bedroom and creaks open the door, but the room she slept in last night is empty. She glances down the shadowy length of the upstairs corridor, but the other bedroom doors are still closed. The only noise is the clawing tap tap tap of a stray branch against a window and the pelting rain on the roof tiles.

Something's wrong. He wouldn't just go off somewhere without leaving a note. Not without the car. Not in this weather. She turns to the window, staring hard through the downpour.

*Shit.*

He'll have gone down to the lake to find her. That's where she had told him she was going. He'd have been worried when she didn't come back before the rain. He'll be soaked through too.

A chill has taken over Anna's body. She's suddenly freezing, the drenching from the rain and the fading adrenaline from her encounter with the old man now combining to sap the life from her. She urgently needs to warm up. In the bathroom she peels off her clinging jeans, then towels the remaining dampness from her hair. But her body has started to shake. She reaches across to turn on the shower and the mirror above the basin instantly fogs with steam. Anna presses the towel against her face and is about to lean in to wipe the mirror when she stops, frozen, the towel suspended.

She is not alone. Someone's downstairs. Her hand reaches for the tap and kills the water. Stock-still, she listens. Her bare feet are damp on the tiled floor as she turns slowly, the towel clutched to her chest, a frightened child seeking comfort from a teddy.

*The back door.*

Her stomach lurches. How could she be so stupid? She left the door unlocked when she went to the lake earlier.

*He's followed her back to the house.*

She pauses at the top stair. In her mind she can clearly see the old man's spittle take flight, can taste his sour breath spill over her face, can feel the phantom jab of broken glass in her lower back. But most of all, she can see his dirty fingers wrapped snug around his blade.

'Dan!'

Anna is whisper-shouting now. If Dan was here he'd definitely have answered her. He knows better than to mess around, knows that Anna would have a total sense of humour failure. She swallows, decides not to call his name again. Her footsteps are cautious on the stairs, her eyes wide. The noise tells her that the man is in the house now. Halfway down the stairs, she crouches. Only metres away, on the far wall of the kitchen, is the magnetic strip of kitchen knives. She has to grab something to defend herself. She drops the towel to her feet and carefully descends the remaining stairs, each step risking a tell-tale creak. With her breath held, she is primed to bolt back up to the bathroom with its lockable door.

She moves to the kitchen, swift and silent, her hand reaching efficiently for the butcher's knife. The handle is cool in her grip as she pulls the blade from the wall holder. She turns, her other hand gripping the handle now too, the knife in front of her body, its sharp tip pointed up, the blade trembling.

Could she do it if she had to? She pictures the old man, his white hair, his craggy face. Could she slash his forearm if he got too close? If he grabbed her could she pierce his gut, puncture his heart? Blood rushes to the surface of her skin, but she feels deathly cold. Her hips press against the edge of the countertop, her body sliding inch by inch. She hasn't thought this through.

Over on the coffee table she spots her phone. She'll grab it, run to the bathroom, call the cops from behind the locked door. But already she knows it's useless. She's in the middle of nowhere. It would take them forever to locate her.

*Think, Anna. Think.*

She could run for the car. But she has no clue where Dan left the keys.

Anna freezes. The noise again. Closer. Much closer. The blade wavers in her sweaty grip, her arms tense. She edges her hip against the counter and prepares to run for her phone on the coffee table. She inhales.

Something bumps her waist. Anna screams.

Dan is struggling past with a heavy cardboard box in one arm. With his free hand he's pulling off his noise-cancelling headphones.

'Sorry. Did I make you jump? Jeez, careful with that knife.'

Tinny music escapes into the air, but Anna can barely hear it above the swoosh of blood in her ears. She wants to punch him. Dan slides the cardboard box onto the kitchen counter, a smug look on his face.

'I didn't realise you were back.'

Behind him, Anna can see the door of the padlocked private room is now ajar. The key from the smashed vase is in the open padlock. Dan kicks the door closed with his boot and the padlock bounces against the wood. It echoes like the padlocked door on the creepy shack in the woods.

Dan places his hands on her shoulders and turns her to face him, his eyebrows knitted as his finger traces her cheek.

'What happened here?'

Anna remembers the graze on her face. 'Oh. I just got lost. Went for a walk and must have scratched it.'

Dan leans in to kiss it better. 'Crazy kid.' He turns his attention back to the cardboard box. He peers inside, humming to himself, happy.

Anna's heart is still pounding, but she watches on curiously as he selects a dusty bottle of red wine and tilts the label to the light.

'Where's the wine from?'

'Hmm?'

'The wine?'

'Oh. Mrs Cassidy.'

'What do you mean?'

'Oh, she wanted to apologise for the mix up with her phone. And for forgetting to arrange the cleaner...'

'Oh. Right. So she gave us a case of wine?'

'Mm hmm.'

Dan continues to study the label.

'Wow.' Anna leans over the box and grabs a random bottle. It's a few years old, French, unfamiliar to her. 'This looks expensive, Dan.'

'Yeah. A nice gesture, huh? I'm looking forward to cracking into it.'

Dan's moved over to the oven now, his back to her. As Anna watches him she feels her heartbeat start to settle. And only now does the aroma of a home-cooked meal begin to pull at her senses. The oven is humming quietly and she remembers Dan's plans to make them a roast dinner.

'So you spoke to her?' Anna sets the bottle back down, a sense that at least something is going right. 'And the cats are good?'

He has slid out the tray of meat and is using a large spoon to baste it.

'What's that?'

Anna watches his back as he fusses over the lamb. She leans on the counter but suddenly wants to touch him, make sure he's real and solid. 'Nip and Tuck. They're okay?'

'Sure. They're good.' He slides the tray back in, closes the oven door and rubs his hands on his jeans. He turns and smiles at her, and that's all it takes. Anna's eyes prickle and a moment later fat teardrops are dripping off her chin.

'Hey, hey. What's all this about?'

He pulls her close and Anna lets herself collapse pathetically into his arms. Her breath is ragged, her limbs weak. Dan's hand cups her scalp and he kisses along her damp hairline.

'It's okay, Banana. It's okay. I'm such a dick. I didn't mean to scare you ...'

She presses herself tighter against his chest. She wants to stay like this forever, safe in his arms. She turns her face slightly, letting her sobs and words escape together.

'A man...'

'What?'

' ... '

'Anna, what are you saying?'

Dan's arms stiffen around her. Something in his stance has instantly set him into warrior mode, her alert protector. 'Tell me.'

She nods mutely into his shoulder, then pushes herself away from him, all of a sudden unsure of herself. She walks to the front door, discretely unlocks it and opens it wide, brave once more. She needs air, sky, perspective.

Dan hovers behind her, but she needs a moment. What will she say? That the old guy they saw yesterday by his caravan threatened her with a stick? Again, she pictures him looming over her as she lay sprawled on her back like a frightened animal. Anna frowns through the rain towards the trees and the narrow path, but with Dan's strong presence behind her the earlier sense of threat seems somewhat confected. She doesn't know what to believe anymore. Since Ger's disappearance she's begun to doubt her own sanity. Did the old man really threaten her?

Dan's hand is on her shoulder again, but this time she doesn't jump. She leans her cheek into the strong ridge of his knuckles.

'What man are you talking about?'

Anna turns. Behind Dan, she can see the low light of the oven and the nice bottle of Mrs Cassidy's red wine he's already selected to accompany the lamb roast. The aroma of his cooking fills the room. Anna opens her mouth but pauses. She thinks back to the lake this afternoon, and the promise she made to herself. For the next few days, until Dan is on the plane, she'll be on her best behaviour. No crazy talk. Nothing to stress him out. Happy memories. Happy Anna.

'It was just that scruffy old guy we saw yesterday. I got a fright running into him in the woods, that's all. You know me, I've been a bit highly strung recently.'

Dan looks off into the distance for a minute, before remembering the mute old codger they drove past on the overgrown laneway yesterday.

'He didn't do anything, did he?'

Anna shakes her head and smiles up at him. 'No, no. Just me being silly.'

The rigidity leaves Dan's body, his warrior mode in retreat. He kisses the top of Anna's head and closes the front door quietly behind her.

'Hey, I've an idea. Why don't you go upstairs and have a bath? You're soaked and you're shivering. I bought some milk earlier. I'll bring you up a cup of tea. Sound good?'

Anna nods. A warming bath and a cup of tea would work wonders on her. But if she's honest with herself, what she really wants right now is to go upstairs, pack their bags and get home to her cats and the familiar creaks and ticks of her and Ger's place. She rests her head for a moment against Dan's shoulder, allowing him to gently rock her back and forth. But she remembers the effort he's going to. She mustn't spoil it. Besides, she has a feeling he has something planned for this evening.

'Okay?'

She pushes back and looks up into his eyes, cajoling her old happy self into making an appearance.

'Better than okay.'

A few minutes later, Anna rests on the edge of the bathtub and slowly plays her hand through the hot sudsy water. From downstairs, a popping sound, as Dan uncorks one of the fancy bottles of red wine. His off-key singing drifts up, bringing a smile to Anna's face. He's spoken to their host and everything's okay, Anna reminds herself, as she lowers herself gingerly into the hot water. The wine was a nice gesture by Mrs Cassidy. The old lady might be a bit forgetful, but she's a generous soul at the end of the day, and that counts for something in Anna's books. The earlier tension in her shoulders is already dissolving in the bathwater as Anna sinks up to her neck. And she remembers the most important thing: Mrs Cassidy confirmed that Ger's cats are fine. That's all Anna had really wanted to know all along. She closes her eyes and slides her body smoothly under the water's surface, all her worries evaporating in the steam.

# July

# SIXTEEN

GER CHECKED HER WATCH for the umpteenth time, a barely touched glass of Guinness warming slowly in front of her. Anna eyed the half bottle of white wine before her on the table. She had no intention of heading yet. Their mates from book club weren't long gone, leaving just Anna and Ger on the bench seat by the window. It had been a cracking summer's day, and now, as Thursday evening progressed, Mulligan's was buzzing.

'Now. Where were we?' Anna took a long sip of her white wine, aiming for distraction. 'Oh yeah, Mexico. Porto something or other.'

After a brief pause, Ger acquiesced with a small sip of her stout. ' *"Porto something"*, my arse. It's Puerto Escondido. Have you talked to your boss yet?'

'I made noises about it last week.' Anna had made no such noises. She had a reminder in her online calendar to talk to Vincent Lynch, her boss at *Houghton, Hartery & Lynch*, about taking four weeks off. But each evening the reminder would be nudged on to the next day.

'Well, flights aren't going to get any cheaper. Come on, Anna. I need to get away and we've been talking about this for ages. I'd have gone on my own already if I'd known you weren't keen. Or invited one of the girls from book club to join me. Have you changed your mind?'

Anna stalled with a long sip of wine. She had been dying to flashpack around Mexico and Guatemala for a month. But with

Dan on the scene nowadays it just didn't hold the same appeal. It was piss-weak to think that way, but the timing wasn't right, not now, not with him here.

'No, no, of course not. I'll talk to the boss next week.'

'Really?'

'I promise. Leave it with me. I'll do it.'

Ger shifted her hips beside Anna on the bench seat, the silence stretching tensely. Maybe they could delay the trip until after Dan headed back to Oz. He'd be gone by October at the latest. Anna took another sip of wine. They hadn't eaten dinner and the booze was going to her head. She nudged Ger's knee with her own.

'So, I can do without air con, but I reckon we'll need ceiling fans.'

Another moment of chilly silence amid the din of the pub, before Ger softened ever-so-slightly beside her.

'I'll need a hammock.' Ger responded, begrudgingly playing along.

'Yes, one each. Overlooking the beach.' Anna held her wine to her chest and leaned into Ger's shoulder. 'And who will be living next to our beach shack in Porto whatchamacallit?'

'Puerto Escondido, you wagon. Well, let's see... to our left we'd have Diego.' Ger was warming to the theme now, Anna's slackness forgiven. 'He plays guitar and runs an animal sanctuary.'

'He'll do. And on the other side?'

'To our right, we'd have recently single surfing philanthropist, Juan. No, Alejandro. Yes, Alejandro, who has come away to our coastal retreat to mend his broken heart.'

'Is he hung?'

'Jeez, Anna. You filthy article.' Ger took another sip. 'Like a horse. We can see into his shower if we stand on tiptoe on our balcony.'

Anna looked down at her own forearm, pink as a Christmas ham and dusted with a smattering of freckles. In contrast, Ger's toned arm, bare from the shoulder in her cream halter neck top, was golden.

'God, Ger, you make me sick sometimes. I wish I had some of your melanin. If I don't want to be red as a beetroot, I'll have to skulk under a parasol and slather myself in Factor 50. It's not fair. You'll be off frolicking with Alejandro and what's his name in the surf.'

'Just imagine. A few weeks where we get to swap the stony shore of the North Strand for soft sand and warm breezes.' Ger said, wistfully. 'Getting away from... from all this.'

Anna glanced sideways at her friend and saw a desperate longing in Ger's face as she disappeared further into her thoughts. Ger did this from time to time, wired their conversations towards travel and other lives in different times and places. It was a clear sign she was stressed, that something wasn't quite right in the here-and-now.

'Sometimes I wonder ... would it not just be easier to disappear.'

Ger's words were barely audible through the din of the bar, but Anna felt a sudden flush of unease.

'Penny for them?'

'Hmm? Oh, nothing.'

'Ger, you should leave that place. They don't—'

'I've no intention of leaving. It will look dodgy if I quit before I have two years under my belt. It's just been a bit awkward recently. That's all.'

Anna took a swig of wine. She knew only too well why it had been awkward. Gavin Sweeney, the watery-faced gobshite, had been pestering Ger again. Actually, harassing was the correct term. Anna hadn't come down in the last shower. She knew harassment existed in myriad forms and that women were conditioned to downplay its impacts to their own detriment. She reached forward to tip the remainder of the wine bottle into her glass, the cheap sauv blanc reaching just shy of the brim. She couldn't imagine working with a knob like Gavin Sweeney, day in, day out, and she struggled to comprehend how a usually self-confident woman like Ger hadn't yet told him to bugger off in front of his leadership team. Ger could walk out tomorrow with her head held high.

'Ah Anna, he's harmless. Just a bit of a creep. I try to make sure I'm not alone with him now. It's fine.'

'Ger, it's not fine. He's taking advantage now that you report to him. Surely there's policies in place? He doesn't ask the others to work late, does he?'

Ger was silent beside her.

'Sorry. That sounded like a criticism.'

'You're grand. I'll leave in a few months, once I get my two years done.' Ger squeezed her knee. 'Try not to worry.'

'Right, enough maudlin talk. Let's forget all that shite. I'm getting you one more for the road.'

'No way. I'm done.' Ger glanced at her watch. 'Bugger. It's gone nine-thirty. These long evenings throw me every time. And we've not eaten.'

'Go on. Another half pint. We'll leave in ten minutes.'

'I can't. I'm up at six thirty in the morning. Gavin's asked me to give a presentation to the Senior Partners at nine. Come on, let's go home. I did say I couldn't do a late one. Leave the wine. It's plonk anyway.' Ger put the novel from book club into her shoulder bag and zipped it up.

'Oh come on, Ger. It's not that late. You'll be in bed by ten thirty.'

Anna nodded out past Ger to the purple streaks of thin cloud raking the sky. Evenings like this couldn't be taken for granted and Anna wasn't ready for bed yet. As Ger hesitated and checked her watch again, Anna bounced on their bench seat like a hyper kid, a leery grin playing over her face.

'Go on, Ger. One more. One more.'

'God, Anna. You'll be the death of me. Okay. One more glass! And let's make it a quick one, yeah?'

'Promise, promise.' Anna held up her right hand as if swearing an oath, and Ger gave up a laugh. Anna stopped abruptly, her own laugh suspended in the air. A cloud had passed across Ger's face and now Anna followed her gaze. Falling in the door were Dan and — Anna's stomach lurched — Gavin Sweeney. Only last month, Dan had told Anna he'd struck up a conversation when he'd been partnered with a guy during a boxing class at the gym. While they'd been chatting they'd worked out they both knew Ger. Now it seemed they'd become drinking buddies. Anna hadn't mentioned it to Ger, in the hope the two guys wouldn't make a habit of it. Now she glanced at Ger, whose face had paled.

'Actually, Anna, I'm pretty knackered. Let's go, hey?' Ger was on her feet.

The lads had spotted them and were approaching, Dan a little glazey-eyed, Gavin looking smug. Anna detected the barest hint of a wobble in Gavin's gait, before she remembered what Ger had told her once about his short leg and the stacked heel on one of his shoes.

'Well, hello ladies.'

Dan leaned in towards Anna for a beery kiss and Anna reached a fingertip to trace the stubble on his cheek. She hadn't seen him in a few days and now the four glasses of wine on an empty stomach had left her frisky. She inhaled his lovely animal warmth.

'Anna. Ger.' Gavin was waiting in the background, a bad smell lingering.

'Hiya Gavin.' Anna kept her voice neutral. There was something sly behind his eyes. The guy made her skin crawl.

'Hi Gavin. Hey Dan.' Ger hung her bag over her shoulder and fixed a loose strand of dark hair behind her ear. 'Shame you guys didn't get here earlier. We're just leaving.'

Ger turned a steady gaze on Anna, an unspoken challenge passing between them. They'd joked in the past about sisters before misters. But right at that moment, Anna couldn't see what harm another drink would do. A moment passed before Ger seemed to realise that Anna had no intention of leaving yet.

'Gentlemen, it looks like I'll be leaving you in Anna's capable hands. I have to go as I'm up early. Big presentation to deliver.' There was a barb in the comment, but it passed over Gavin's head. Ger sidled out just beyond the two men, further away from Anna. It was pointless to encourage her to stay, yet Anna heard her own words, whiny and childlike.

'Ah, one more, Ger. Go on. Just one more.'

Even in her tipsy state, Anna couldn't mistake the flash of annoyance on Ger's face. She'd seen this expression before, the day they'd planned to meet Ger's brother, Lorcan, and his wife in town. That same day Dan had turned up unannounced, and Anna had failed to follow Ger into town on the later train. Now, Anna watched Ger turn and squeeze through the throng of regulars. Dan had signalled to the barman for a pint and had plonked himself down beside Anna at their table. Anna glanced back towards the door as Ger exited into the evening.

'Well, you know what they say,' Gavin stated. 'Two's company…'

He hovered at the edge of the table, forcing Anna to pretend to look for a mint in her bag.

'Sit down, Gav. Relax.' Dan was scooting Anna further up along the bench.

'Nah. I'll go out for a ciggie, then hit the road. See you soon.'

Anna sensed him looking at her, but she avoided his eyes, focusing on a showy cufflink as he draped his jacket over his shoulder. Dan nudged her, so she flashed a tight smile past his left ear and exhaled in relief as the creep navigated the crowds towards the exit.

'Prick.' She said it quietly enough, not wanting to waste any more energy talking about Gavin Sweeney, and leaned her body in towards Dan. As he began to tell her about his day, Anna struggled to pay attention, Dan's words drifting, the wine dulling her senses. She turned her face slightly, so she could subtly glance over his shoulder. Ger was walking up the street, her cream halter neck top catching the remnants of the evening light. Anna lifted her big glass of wine and took a generous sip. When Dan showed her something on his phone, Anna guessed an appropriate response and grunted in agreement. But her eye was soon drawn back to the window. She craned her neck. Further up the street, a filthy white van had slowed to a crawl by the pavement. Anna could just about make out Ger. She had stopped to talk to the driver. Perhaps it was someone looking for directions.

Anna turned back to her wine and took another swig. A strange sense of discomfort had started to wash through her gut. She shouldn't drink any more, not on an empty stomach. Her hand reached for her bag beside her on the bench, her fingers playing distractedly over its scuffed leather surface. She could still catch Ger if she left right now. Dan would be happy on his own. She shouldn't be a sketchy friend.

But the evening light had shifted while she dithered, and when Anna looked out the window once again, the street was deserted, no Ger, no van. She nestled back into the familiarity of Dan's shoulder, seeking comfort in the baritone of his voice.

*Ger's a big girl*, Anna reminded herself. *She'll be halfway home by now.*

# October

# SEVENTEEN

ANNA DABS THE CORNER OF HER MOUTH with a napkin and looks down at her empty plate.

'Dan, you've surpassed yourself. That was absolutely delicious.'

She lifts her empty plate and reaches across for Dan's too.

'Sit down, love. I'm clearing up.'

'But you cooked ...'

'But nothing. Now, sit there. Don't move.'

He's on his feet, taking the plates from her and carrying them over to the sink. Anna sinks back into her chair and discreetly pops open the top button on her jeans. Between the pub lunch earlier and the roast dinner now, she's not eaten this much in months and her hunger has surprised her. Dan has lit a candle in an old wine bottle and the flickering flame softens the edges of the room. As Anna stares at the flame, she feels her own edges softening too, the ever-present tension melting from her neck and shoulders. She is bathed, fed and relaxed. Tonight she will entertain no arguments in her head with Sergeant Rooney, there will be no lingering resentment towards the rude woman at the bar earlier, or flashes of fear when she thinks of the old man in the woods with his knife. They can all take the night off and just give Anna some peace. She glances over to the open fridge where Dan is sliding something out.

'Ta da!'

He turns towards her and holds up a bottle of champagne and two glasses.

'Now I know you've not been drinking since …' He clears his throat and moves towards her. 'But I figured you might make an exception tonight.'

Anna opens her mouth to protest but is too curious to interrupt him. She sits upright, forcing herself out of her food coma. Dan has put the champagne and glasses on the table and is pulling his chair in closer towards her. She shifts on her seat again. Dan's eyes are locked on hers as he slides an envelope across the table until the paper is resting under her fingertips. Anna looks down and frowns back up at Dan.

'Go on,' he smiles. 'Open it.'

Anna's fingers work carefully over the envelope, clueless as to the contents. She slides out a folded sheet of paper, and tilts it towards the candlelight, straining to read it.

'Dan. Is this—'

Her eyes search his smiling face for confirmation, and then she studies the printout again. She reaches for her water glass and drains the last dribble.

'It's a ticket to Oz.' Dan leans forward and takes her free hand in his. 'When I board that plane on Thursday morning, I want you in the seat beside me.'

'But …'

'It's just for a month, see?' He indicates a return date on the page, but the characters are dancing in Anna's vision. Dan continues, 'I know it's a surprise. But I've been thinking about it for ages. I would have mentioned it sooner, but, well, you know …'

Anna does know. That's his subtle way of saying she's been a headcase for the past three months. She looks at the champagne bottle. A trickle of condensation runs down its length and she feels a sudden need for a drink.

'My sister has a place in Sydney, at Tamarama. She's offered it to us while she's overseas. Just the two of us, a five-minute walk to the beach. You'll love it there. You can swim every day. And I figure we could do a bit of a road trip too, maybe even take you up to my Dad's farm …'

Anna lets Dan talk, the sound of the rain drumming against the roof and the dancing candle flame adding something surreal to his words. As he rubs his thumb tip over the back of her hand, he paints her a picture of big blue skies and the world's best beaches, cockatoos and kookaburras, eucalypts and jacarandas.

Anna stares at the print-out. Her full name in bold capital letters, the flight codes and departure times. Dan has stopped talking. He's watching her, his raised eyebrows encouraging her to speak. 'Dan, I don't know what … I think I'm in shock.'

There's a film of cold sweat on her skin and Anna wonders if he can feel it on her hand. She has the good sense to flash him a smile, but she's aware of something crumbling deep inside herself. She can barely breathe. This isn't how it's meant to be. She should be thrilled, shouting a definitive yes to the heavens. He's waiting, the moment dragging.

Anna opens her mouth, no clue what to say, when a familiar ring tone pierces the air. They look over to the kitchen counter where Dan's mobile buzzes and flashes in the darkness. Dan smirks at Anna but holds his position.

'Dan, maybe you should—'

But he's waiting, his hand still clasping Anna's, until his phone falls silent again.

'Now, where were we? What do you say, Banana? Will you come back with me?'

'Dan, I—'

His phone shrills again. Dan stands, annoyance flashing on his face as he crosses to the kitchen. He stares at the screen for just a second too long before jabbing the Reject button.

'Who is it, Dan?'

'Hmm?'

Anna stands, a sudden need to move, her limbs twitchy. As she walks towards him he pockets the phone in the back of his jeans.

'What's that?'

'I said who was it?'

'Oh, that, just one of the lads from work. Probably wanting to go for a goodbye pint. Now, let's try again?'

Dan gently tugs Anna's hand in the direction of her chair once more, but she finds herself rooted to the spot, surveying the dimly lit kitchen, and glancing over to the coffee table and sofas.

'Where's my phone?' She extracts her hand from Dan's and clicks on the floor lamp near the coffee table, the room ugly once more. 'Have you seen it anywhere?'

Behind her, Dan sighs.

'I put it away.'

Anna turns to face him. He looks sheepish and defiant in equal measure. 'You put it away?'

'I put it away. I didn't want us to be disturbed.'

'Right.' Anna looks past him to the candle flame, now redundant in the glare of the lamp. 'So where is it?' He doesn't answer her, and when she looks up there's an expression of incredulous frustration blooming on his face.

'For Christ's sake, Anna. I'm in the middle of asking you to come back to Australia with me and you urgently need to check your phone? Are you for real?'

There's a sudden flash of heat in Anna's chest and her jaw tightens. She stares at the sweating champagne bottle and for a fleeting moment wants more than anything to sweep it off the table with her arm.

'Give me my phone, Dan.'

'Sweet Jesus, Anna. You're a fucking addict.'

'I want my phone, Dan.' She keeps her tone even, her hand outstretched, her eyes on the champagne bottle.

'Of course you want your phone, Anna. You're like a junkie needing a fix. Do you know how many times I've woken in the middle of the night to see you checking your precious phone?'

'How dare you. You know what I'm doing. I'm checking the news. I'm checking the missing persons database. I'm—'

'How could I not know? It's the first thing you reach for in the morning and the last thing you look at each night. It's like a sickness, Anna.'

'Shut up!' She's pacing the room, her hands balled, the hateful threat of tears not far off.

'We can't even have a meal together without you tapping out another message to that bloody cop. I feel sorry for the guy. God forbid your Sergeant Rooney tries to have a life outside of work.'

Anna stops, her body a tight coil. She could take a swing at him, right now, catch him unawares and watch him stagger backwards into the table. He mistakenly takes her silence as her yielding to his viewpoint. When he next speaks he sounds somewhat conciliatory.

'Listen, it's only because I care about you. I just wanted us to have a conversation, without any interruptions, you know? It's been a crappy few months and I'm trying to save us.' Something cracks in his voice, a damn on the point of breaking. 'It's our last Saturday together, Banana.' He looks over at the print-out on the dining table. 'Well … maybe. I dunno … '

Anna stares, unblinking, into the middle distance. She needs to take a moment to slow her breathing, to calm herself, to be a grown-up.

'Dan?'

'Yes, love.' He moves towards her.

'You're a fucking idiot.' Anna surprises herself with the venom in her delivery. He has stopped abruptly, shocked and stung.

'My best friend is missing and you expect me to swan off on holiday with you? Are you cracked in the head? Only three months after Ger ...' Her throat is tightening, her voice rising, something deep and dark unleashed. 'Can you imagine what her poor parents would think? What planet are you on?'

Dan has taken a step back. He's watching her as if she's a demented stranger. 'Far out, Anna. You really—'

'You don't get to manipulate me. Ever! Do you understand? If I want to check my phone, I'll check my bloody phone.'

Anna throws him a disgusted look and races up the stairs, letting her next words trail over her shoulder.

'Enjoy the sofa. You absolute prick!'

She slams the bedroom door. Her breath is heavy, her eyes have started to sting. Outside, there's a momentary pause in the rain, but no moonlight penetrates the cloud. Anna slides her back down the door until she comes to rest on the carpet.

*Oh Anna*, she groans to herself as she hugs in her knees and rests her forehead, squeezing her damp eyes shut against the world. And in that moment, in the settling stillness, she wishes more than anything that Ger was here to wrap a comforting arm around her.

# July

# EIGHTEEN

THE POLICE STATION IN SKERRIES had the air of a proud home rather than somewhere a criminal might be charged. An end-of-terrace two-storey building in the heart of the village, neat hedges framed the front lawn and borders of pink flowers lined the well-swept path. Baskets of petunias, pansies and fuchsias sat proud on each windowsill. The only hint of what lay behind the facade was a blue Garda beacon, reminiscent of a Victorian London streetlamp, fixed to the wall. The navy colour of the beacon perfectly matched the paintwork of the heavy front door. But the pretty facade of the building was lost on Anna that morning as she marched up the path with Dan in tow. She didn't want to be here, doing what she was about to do.

Anna's heart sank as she pushed through the door to find a slightly plump desk sergeant who looked like she should be at home doing her chemistry homework. Behind the girl, a mirrored partition concealed the goings-on from the general public. The desk sergeant, free of make-up, had her brown hair combed back into a tight ponytail. She looked up from her mobile phone and smiled at Anna, then let her gaze linger on Dan before turning her attention back to the worried looking woman in front of her. Anna took a deep breath.

'I need to report a missing person.'

The cop regarded her, unblinking for a moment, and Anna wondered if she was struggling to dredge up the appropriate process from her time at police academy.

'Right. Okay. Well, first things first, let's start with a few details.'

That look again, fleeting, but she was taking in Dan. Anna found herself shuffling a few inches to her right, blocking her view.

'Name please.'

'Ger. Short for Geraldine. Ger Kelly.'

'Okay, Ger. And can I grab some contact—'

'No.'

'No?'

'No. Sorry. I mean, Ger is my friend. She's the one who is missing. My name is Anna. Anna Moriarty.'

This shouldn't be so difficult, but Anna had a shit night's sleep. Her left hand flailed behind her until Dan's fingers found it. He stepped forward so that they presented a united front.

'Okay. Anna. And Sir?'

'You want my details too?'

'Yes.'

Anna forced herself to breathe. If this young woman mentioned Dan's accent or started chatting about Vegemite or Kylie Minogue or her time spent backpacking up the East coast of Australia, she couldn't be sure she wouldn't slam her head into the desk.

Dan cleared his throat and leaned forward. The poor guy couldn't have got much sleep either, with Anna tossing and turning all night. His eyes had dark circles too.

'Dan. Daniel. Daniel Pell.'

'Right Daniel. Thank you. And thank you Anna. So, tell me a few details about ...' She glances at the form, 'Ger, is it? Have you tried her phone? Contacted anyone she lives with?'

'She hasn't answered her phone. We live together.'

'Are you partners?'

'Partners? No, no we're friends and we share a house. Daniel here is my partner.'

'Right.'

Daniel's hand squeezed Anna's gently, his thumb tracing her knuckles.

'So, Anna, when did you last see Ger?'

Anna's mouth was suddenly parched. This was surreal, wheels now officially in motion, a *Missing Persons* form taking shape in front of her. A flash of doubt arose. She was going to find Ger at home later, the dirty stopout having met an old boyfriend on her way home from the pub on Thursday, smelling of sex and revelling in her recklessness, and apologising to Anna for causing such a fuss. And although Anna might feign annoyance with her best friend, inwardly she'd collapse with gratitude.

'Thursday. Thursday night just after nine thirty. She left Mulligan's bar——'

'Mulligans?' The cop frowned up at the ceiling corner for a moment. 'The pub down on Holmpatrick, big front window, that the one?'

'That's the one, yes.'

'And you were out together.'

'We were. Book club. Drinks. Ger had a big day at work on Friday, so she wanted to leave.'

'And she left the pub alone?'

Anna swallowed and stared down at the form. The pen had stopped moving. The young woman's eyes were on her. She nodded, mute, a hateful itch at the back of her eyes.

'Yes. She left alone.'

'Okay. Now, Ger's employer. Has anyone confirmed if she turned up to work on Friday? You said she had a big day?'

'We rang her boss this morning. It's not unusual for Ger to work late, so when I went to bed last night I thought she had come in at some stage after a long day at the office. But I checked her room this morning. She hadn't been home. And that's when we rang Gavin. He's her manager. He confirmed she was a no-show in the office yesterday. Gavin. Gavin Sweeney.'

The pen hovered, but the cop wasn't committing his name to paper. Anna chewed on her bottom lip, then leaned forward.

'Gavin was there in the pub on Thursday. He left just after Ger did. She'd been having issues with him at work. Harassment and stuff ...'

Dan had turned to look at her, but in that moment Anna didn't care. The slimy prick needed to be checked out. The pen started moving again, and when the cop asked for Gavin's work details and phone number Anna was only too happy to furnish them.

Behind the mirrored screen a man's voice rose, a thick Dub accent, before crashing into a throaty laugh which gave way to a smoker's cough. The policewoman looked up at Anna and offered her a tight-lipped smile. She took other details too, their address and phone numbers, Ger's next of kin, her age, height and social media accounts, her medical history and mood. She slowly looked over the form, careful not to omit anything, the nib of her pen hovering. Anna drummed her fingers on the desk and the young woman looked up.

'Nearly done, folks. Anna, can you give me a description of what Ger was wearing?'

Anna described Ger's outfit, clearly picturing the halter-neck top and its creamy contrast against her brown arms as Ger walked away from the pub in the dying shards of evening light.

'There was a van.'

'What's that?'

Anna felt Dan's eye upon her again. She glanced from him back to the cop, the memory only coming back to her now. She latched on, scouring her fuggy synapses.

'A white van. Outside the pub. I looked out as Ger was heading up the street. This van slowed beside her and she stopped to lean in, to talk to the person.' The words spilled out in a manic rush. The man who'd been hidden behind the mirrored partition had poked his head around to ask the desk sergeant something, but on hearing Anna he moved slowly towards the counter. He was middle-aged, tall and lithe but for his little pot belly. He maintained a respectable distance but was clearly listening to Anna's every word. For some reason she wanted to impress this man, needed him to take this seriously.

'I don't suppose you got their number plate?' Ponytail had her eyebrows raised hopefully.

Anna shook her head. She wanted to tell her she had had five glasses of white wine, or was it six, and nothing to eat by that stage of the night. But she thought better of it.

'And the direction of travel?'

'Well, it was heading up in this direction.'

'Okay. North. Can you think of anything else, Anna? Anything, no matter how irrelevant it might seem?'

Anna leaned her elbows on the desk and scrunched shut her eyes, her forehead resting heavily against her hands. Her body was exhausted but her brain was wired. She was trying her best not to imagine Ger bound and gagged and utterly terrified in the back of a van somewhere.

'Tinted windows! I'm pretty sure it had tinted windows.'

'Okay. Good, that helps. So, from what you're telling me, Ger was last seen outside Mulligan's just after nine thirty on Thursday evening. When you checked her bedroom this morning, that's when you became concerned and called her boss, Gavin, and learned she hadn't shown up to work yesterday. And the last interaction you're aware of is with the driver of a white van with tinted windows, outside Mulligans. Does that sound fair?'

'Yes.'

'Daniel?'

'Eh, yes. Yes. I didn't see the van myself. But everything else, yes.'

The desk sergeant turned to the pot-bellied man. Something wordless passed between them. Anna risked a proper look at him now. He was in his mid-fifties and had the look of someone keen for early retirement, his own dark circles probably a more permanent feature than Dan's. She spotted something poking out of his trouser pocket, a vape, perhaps, and remembered his smoker's cough. He moved closer to the counter now and took the Missing Persons form from the desk sergeant. They all remained silent as he read it.

'Anna, Daniel? I'm Sergeant Rooney. Would you be able to bring in a recent photograph of Ger?'

In a flash, Anna had her bag open and had slapped down the photograph from the broken frame in the kitchen. Sergeant Rooney gave her an impressed nod, then tilted it towards the window. It was the picture Dan took the first day he met them both, Anna and Ger leaning into each other. Anna felt nauseous looking at it now. By tomorrow, half the country might very well be seeing a cropped version of this picture on the evening news.

Sergeant Rooney was making a slow clucking noise with his tongue.

'I know this woman. At least, I've seen her around the village.'

Ponytail leaned in closer, as if she was suddenly going to recognise Ger too.

'Didn't she come in here once, with her clipboard, wanting us to sign a petition?' Now it was Sergeant Rooney's turn to frown up at the ceiling corner while he wracked his brains.

'She did,' he agreed with himself now. 'A petition objecting to that new hotel being built on the Balbriggan Road. That's right. I wasn't going to sign it, but she convinced me.' He chortled to himself, then looked at the photo in his hand with renewed interest and a hint of admiration.

Anna cleared her throat and he looked up. 'Sergeant Rooney, this isn't like Ger, you know?' She held his stare, unblinking, needing him to take her seriously.

He nodded slowly. He got it. But then his eyes moved over to Dan and stayed on him for a while. Anna realised he was taking stock of them both, seeing them as potential suspects, the reason Ger had vanished without a trace. When his gaze returned to Anna, something softened in his eyes, and she found herself wondering if this lanky, pot-bellied smoker in front of her had daughters of his own.

'My advice to you both is go home, get some rest. Keep your phones charged and turned on, just in case Ger tries to contact you.' He slid a card across the desk to Anna and tapped it twice with a nicotine-stained finger. 'These are my details. If you hear anything, please alert us immediately. In the meantime, we'll start the ball rolling.'

Anna picked up the card and nodded. Beside her, Dan shuffled his feet and turned to leave. His hand was touching the small of her back. But something prevented Anna from moving. She needed something else from these people, a promise that Ger would be found safe and sound and dropped off at their front door later today. But the desk sergeant had turned to a computer to type up the Missing Persons form, and Sergeant Rooney had headed off behind the mirrored partition again.

'Come on, Banana.'

Dan had opened the front door of the station and a warm breeze carried in the faint perfume of the window baskets outside. Anna stared at the desk and nodded, numb and useless. She let Dan's hand guide her away from the desk.

'Anna?'

She turned, momentarily startled. Sergeant Rooney was leaning out from behind the partition.

'We'll find her, okay?'

Anna nodded, and lifted a hand in silent acknowledgement, no longer trusting herself with words. And as she stepped out through the doorway into the glare of the mid-morning sun, an eerie premonition echoed through her body: this wouldn't be Anna's last time crossing this threshold.

# NINETEEN

FOUR DAYS HAD PASSED SINCE the police report had been filed, but to Anna each passing hour had stretched like an eternity. Dan had been staying over every night, but tonight he'd decided to sleep in his own place, probably now smoking weed and playing on the X-box with his two backpacker flatmates. Anna couldn't blame him. The guy had shadows under his eyes to match Anna's, her nocturnal screaming fits waking them both in the dead of night. It would do them no harm to have a night apart, Anna had told herself, as Dan headed out the front door earlier. But by this evening she knew she had to get out for a walk, the needy cats doing her head in, the utter tripe on the telly unable to distract her from the crushing sense of claustrophobia within her own four walls. She walked purposefully, sure to stick to the back streets and quiet lanes of the village. She was in no mood to run into anyone.

*Shit.*

Sinéad from book club had just rounded the corner and had already spotted Anna. Even from the twenty or so metres separating them, the woman's usual frown line was deepening with every no-nonsense forward step. Anna steeled herself for an unwelcome hug, her eyes focusing on the large hoop earrings, anything to avoid *that look*. Anna bristled as the arms enveloped her and a hand patted her shoulder blade. Why did they all want to coo and claw and pull her in for useless clammy embraces while spouting worse-than-useless platitudes?

'Anna! Oh love, you look wrecked. Come here to me.'

The smell of damp wool filled Anna's nostrils as her chin came to momentarily rest on Sinéad's bony shoulder. Then her body was pushed back to arm's length, affording Sinéad a good old gawp.

'You poor thing.' She was clucking and tutting now. 'Did you not get my messages? I've been phoning you. We've been worried sick...'

Anna forced herself to look back at her friend's face, registered the concern, but detected something else too, something which brought to mind Ger's last expression just before she left the pub on Thursday night. Disappointment. That was it. Anna had become the queen of disappointment.

'I'm sorry, Sinéad. I—'

It came from nowhere. At first, a little tightening of the throat, then the subtlest of stings behind the eyes. Anna caught herself, stiffened her shoulders and stood tall. None of them understood. If she removed just one brick from the wall it would all come tumbling down. She needed to be strong. Ger was depending on her.

Sinéad began to say something, no doubt a nugget of wisdom that might just steer Anna into safer waters. But Anna wasn't listening. Instead she stared horrified at the telegraph pole a couple of metres away. Last night she'd gone around the village with a new batch of *Missing Person* posters, laminated this time to withstand the elements. Now she looked at the picture of Ger, the laminated A4 page flapping in the breeze rushing up from the shore. Some little bastard had used a marker pen to draw a moustache and some devil horns on Ger's lovely face. Anna pushed Sinéad away and whipped down the poster.

'Anna?'

But already Anna was blustering herself away down the street, a quick hand raised in silent farewell, Sinéad's bewildered concern trailing after her. Sweet Jesus, had they no respect? It was probably just some bored teenagers, but Ger was one of their own. Someone's daughter. Someone's sister. Someone's friend. She was Someone in her own right. Anna rolled the poster into a tight tube and gripped it like a baton, unable to just chuck it in a bin. People could be so cruel. She rubbed the back of her hand roughly over her eyes, her hair wild in the wind. The headlights from a homeward-bound commuter swept over her face as the car took the roundabout. Two guys smoking outside the chippie nudged each other into silence as she passed. Anna didn't care. Let them all stare and judge her in her messy devastation. As she walked on past shuttered shopfronts, she extracted a balled-up tissue from her sleeve and blew her nose. The darkening streets had grown quiet, the only signs of life the sound of family mealtimes and snippets of TV shows leaking out through the odd open window. She tried hard not to think as she marched on, knowing that she had to work hard to control her mood. But an ever present guilt had been constantly traipsing after her since last week, a bad-tempered puppy nipping at her ankles, growing surlier by the day. She'd give anything now to just turn back the clock, to leave the pub with her best friend as they'd agreed. If only it was that simple. With spectacular timing, Anna looked up to find herself just coming into view of Mulligan's pub across the road. A cheery bunch of friends sat drinking on the other side of the large windowpane, carefree and blessed, a different lifetime ago for Anna. She stumbled slightly as it dawned on her: she was passing the exact spot where she'd last seen Ger at the white van. Now some tears did escape her eyes. She picked up her pace as a snatch of laughter escaped the pub when the door momentarily swung open. Anna suddenly needed to be home, desperate for the cats and the telly and the privacy afforded by her own four walls.

She turned right onto Millers Lane. To her left was the old stone wall bordering Holmpatrick cemetery. She focused her gaze on the pavement one metre in front of her feet. She wouldn't look in towards the cemetery, no matter how much it called to her now. She'd never know if Ger had taken a shortcut through there that night, but right now—

A sound behind her. Had she just heard footsteps? Fine hairs rose on the back of Anna's neck and her jacket felt tight across her chest. She walked on, struggling to keep her pace even, forcing herself not to draw attention to herself. She was just being silly, nobody was following her. Across the road, the houses and gardens sat in silence. It would just be a dog walker, or some innocent on their way home. Someone, just like Anna, who had every right to be walking in public on a Wednesday night. She'd just glance over her shoulder, take a moment to confirm it was nothing to worry about. But something was stopping her from looking around, a fear that a glance would alert whoever was back there.

Anna halted. Whatever noise was behind her stopped abruptly too. She turned slowly, then took a tentative step back in the direction from which she'd just come. Had someone just ducked out of sight? Her eyes squinted through the gloom. She couldn't be sure, but she saw something. A man, just where the old cemetery wall curved away to the right? Anna reached out the fingers of her right hand, her fingertips grazing the rough stone wall, and forced one foot in front of the other. Her walk became a trot, then her feet moved faster still, her left hand gripping tight on the *Missing Persons* scroll. She kept her eye fixed on the farthest point of the curving wall, certain someone was there, moving away from her, just out of sight. The canopy of an old oak tree blocked out the weak illumination from the overhead streetlight.

'Hey!' she shouted into the darkness. She picked up speed, her heart pounding. What the hell would she do if he came at her? Her eyes struggled to separate the moving shadows from the blurred edges of the wall. 'Stop!' Somewhere a dog barked. 'Stop, I said!'

Suddenly, the toe of Anna's left foot clipped an uneven patch of kerb. She stumbled, her momentum too much to save her. She scrunched her eyes closed, somehow managing to protect her face with her free hand as she tumbled. The air was punched from her lungs as her body hit the pavement. She lay there, temporarily winded, a nasty sting of gravel in her hand and knee. A leftover puddle from a shower this afternoon started to seep into her sleeve, but she remained there, pulling in air, momentarily entranced by the proximity of the slick tarmac to her face. In the background, the dog began to bark again. A light flicked on out the front of one of the houses across the road. An elderly couple stood tentatively on their doorstep, the woman nudging the man to go across and check on the human heap on the ground. Anna tried to move, but the effort seemed gargantuan. She took in a deep breath and used her stinging hand to push her face a few inches off the pavement. In the near distance, a car engine loomed closer. She glanced back up the road towards the curve in the old wall and wondered if her stalker was still there, lurking, or maybe he'd hopped the wall into the cemetery and was observing her from the shadows of an ivy-strewn headstone. The headlights of the car swung around the curve and a moment later the brakes squealed to a halt a few metres in front of her. Anna staggered herself upright, held up a hand to shield her eyes from the glare of the beams. On the ground, the scrolled up *Missing Person* poster had unfurled and was slowly spinning like a child's sad toy in the puddle.

'Anna?'

A man's voice, familiar. Anna walked over and squinted in through the passenger window to the driver.

*Gavin Sweeney.*

Anna's hand tightened on the side of the car.

'Anna, it is you. Are you al—'

'Get away from me, you bastard!'

'What…?' His ferrety mouth opened, then closed again.

A hot rage surged through Anna's veins. She could prove nothing, but in her gut she knew the man in front of her had something to do with Ger's disappearance. He reached for the auto lock button a split second before Anna yanked at the door handle.

'You're a bastard, Sweeney!' Anna tugged at the door handle again. 'You know where she is!'

The elderly couple across the road had come down to the bottom of their driveway, leaning into each other, concern etched on their faces. Anna didn't care. In fact it was better to have witnesses. Another car had come to a halt behind Gavin's and one coming in the other direction had slowed to a crawl, kids in the back pressed up against the glass.

Anna stepped back and kicked at the wing mirror, her foot connecting in rhythm to her words.

'You!'

*Kick*

'Fucking!'

*Kick*

'Monster!'

*Kick*

With her last kick the mirror snapped back, then smacked against the paintwork. Anna leaned forward with her hands on her hips, catching her breath for a moment, before wiping the back of her hand across her mouth. Across the road the elderly woman had brought her fingers to her forehead to bless herself. The husband was pulling her back towards the safety of their house. Anna glanced to the road. A mobile phone was being held out the window of the car behind. Someone was recording it all.

With a sudden squeal of tyres, Gavin Sweeney floored his little shit box up the road. Anna watched it disappear and shook her head at his spinelessness. The other two cars crawled slowly onward, the mobile phone still trained on the mad woman. Anna gave the owner the finger as it passed. Might as well make it worth their while. She might even go viral.

Alone once more, she reached for the laminated poster where it had fallen on the ground, then shook off the rainwater. A light drizzle had started to fall and she flipped up her collar. But as she turned for home, ploughing up the deserted pavement, she couldn't help but cast another glance over her shoulder, a lingering sixth sense that someone still watched from the shadows.

# October

# TWENTY

DAN STARES AT THE DRIPPING TAP in the kitchen. The shower upstairs has spluttered into life and he's sorely tempted to blast the cold water down here so Anna gets scalded. He stares at the tap a moment longer, before dismissing the petty idea with a shake of his head. He heads up the stairs and begins to ram his few items of clothing back into his weekend bag. As he jogs back down the stairs with the bag thrown over his shoulder, a familiar twinge echoes through his lumbar region.

*Great.*

A second shit night's sleep on that prolapsed sofa has stuffed up his spine and he'll have to make a last-minute appointment with a physio. Just what he needs this close to a twenty-four-hour journey crammed into an economy seat.

Over on the coffee table, the print-out containing Anna's flight details looks accusingly back at him in the cool light of day. What was he thinking? He grunts at his stupidity, his thankless attempt at bringing some much-needed happiness into the bloody woman's life flung back in his face. He heads for the front door with his bag and stops abruptly when he opens it, taken aback by a thick wall of mist outside. He can see neither ground nor sky but can feel the cold dampness suspended in the air. He walks out blindly into the mist and zaps the car, the flash of the taillights barely penetrating the grey soup all around. He throws his bag into the boot and slams it shut, leaving his hand to rest on the cool metal for a moment. What would happen if he just drove out of this hellhole right now, if he left Anna here to make her own way home? He closes his eyes and exhales slowly. He couldn't do that to her. But Christ, he's tempted. He's dreading the two-hour drive back to Skerries this morning.

As he reaches the front door he stops and turns, aware for the first time of the utter silence. Last night's storm has moved off, its energy spent, nothing moving now. No branches or leaves stir overhead, no ravens caw, the world around him is in absolute stillness. Already the car has been swallowed up by the mist again and it occurs to Dan that they might struggle to find the overgrown dirt track back out of the property. He heads inside and kicks the front door closed.

The milky light coming in through the dirty windows makes the dingy living room even more depressing. He rolls his shoulders back, a needling tension stuck in between his shoulder blades. He can't wait to get out of here, away from the lumpy sofa, the dead plants, the grimy surfaces and the tired decor. The weekend has been nothing short of a disaster. At least they did the world a service by getting rid of the fugly vase. He allows himself a sly smile at this.

His thoughts turn to the little dipshit who's really caused this mess in the first place. Sad little Hopalong, piggybacking on his dead stepmother's house swap account. Threatening their cats. Getting up to God-knows-what at Anna's cottage. Dan tilts his head and rubs either side of his temple. What a total clusterfuck. He glances at his watch. It's just gone eight a.m. If Anna gets her arse in gear they could be on the road in five minutes and be home around ten if the Sunday morning roads are empty. He'll drop Anna at the shops when they arrive at Skerries, ask her to pick up something for lunch, then he'll whizz home and surprise the little shit. Dan cracks his knuckles as he imagines storming up to the bedroom to find the freak passed out in yesterday's clothes and reeking of stale booze. He'll wake him with the toe of his boot and enjoy the look of confusion on his spotty little face. And then Dan will get to work on him with his fists.

He takes out his pouch of tobacco and sprinkles some chopped weed onto a skin, deftly rolling a thick joint as he listens to Anna moving around upstairs. He's about to step out the back door, then stops. Why the hell should he bother smoking outside? A waft of weed will probably improve the stale smell of this dump of a place. He plonks himself down on the sofa and picks up his laptop, needing a distraction, as he sparks up the joint. His fingers open up the house swap website and his eyes rove over the message history. He won't look at the video of the cats again. The memory of that alone is enough to send his blood pressure surging. He starts typing a response he has no intention of sending. He's not a fool, and if this thing was to get legal he sure as hell doesn't want anything incriminating in writing. But in the absence of being able to beat the crap out of the guy for another couple of hours, he'll vent by typing a message in the meantime. He takes a long toke on the spliff and cracks his fingers again.

> *Hey Mrs Cassidy. Or should I say Hopalong?*
> *How you going, shithead?*
> *You're dead, you scummy little prick.*
> *I just hope you're able to eat hospital food with broken fingers.*
> *You're gonna wish you hadn't fucked with me, ya runty freak.*

The pointy knot of anger in Dan's chest throbs but doesn't appear to be sated. He takes another long draw on the joint, the burning tip flaring as he inhales. He glances to the dining table and a smile twists up the corners of his mouth as he spots the case of wine. He polished off a bottle by himself last night, a damn nice drop it was too. The rest of the case will be coming back with them. Dan smirks across at the padlock on the private storage room and continues to type.

> *By the way, I went somewhere I shouldn't have.*
> *Made a nice little discovery on your property.*
> *Ooops ;-)*

Dan looks at the words on the screen. He's not stupid, but the same vengeful part of him that wanted to scald Anna with hot water a moment ago now lets his index finger hang playfully over the *SEND* button. The shower has stopped. He'll finish his smoke before she comes down. As he's taking a greedy pull on the joint the flaring tip breaks off and drops onto the keyboard.

*Shit!*

He flicks the burning ash off the keyboard with the side of his hand, then blows any remnants onto the crummy sofa. A door closes upstairs. Anna's on her way. As Dan leans forward to place the laptop back on the coffee table he pauses. His stomach clenches. The words he didn't mean to send have been sent. His finger must have brushed the send key.

He sits rigid for a moment on the edge of the sofa, then slowly lowers the joint to the carpet where he stubs it out under the heel of his shoe.

*It doesn't really matter, does it? The little prick probably won't be up for a few hours.*

Dan glances at the laptop once more, a rumbling of unease in the depths of his belly, then closes it over, just as Anna's foot creaks on the top stair. He takes a deep breath as he stands, inwardly preparing for World War III, then moves to the bottom of the staircase.

Immediately he is crushed by remorse. Anna looks dreadful, her face more hollowed out than normal. Her downcast eyes are bloodshot and are not yet able to meet his gaze. He exhales, remembering what he should be focusing on, his woman, standing helpless before him. He takes a small step forward, his voice soft in the stillness.

'How you doing?'

Anna remains on the bottom stair, her fingers unwilling to release the banister rail. Her hair is still wet from the shower and lies lank over the collar of her dressing gown. A slight shrug of her shoulders is all she can muster in response. Dan takes another step towards her.

'Listen, Banana. I think we both said some things last night that maybe we shouldn't have …'

Her low gaze is taking in the room now. She stares vacantly across to the open cool box on the kitchen counter which Dan still needs to fill with their remaining food from the fridge.

'This place …' Dan glances around the gloom and shakes his head. '… it's not what I had in mind for our last weekend together. I stuffed up. I'm sorry.'

She's nodding silently, her eyes brimming with tears. He closes the short distance between them, Anna still on the bottom stair, and feels her collapse into him, lets her heave and sob silently against his shoulder.

'Shush. It's okay.' He cups her damp scalp with his hand. 'We'll hit the road as soon as you're dressed. Get you back to your own bed and you can snuggle with the two cats. Does that sound good?'

Dan glances discreetly at his watch. She's nodding into his shoulder. There are words as well, but they're muffled, so he takes a step back and fixes a loose strand of her wet hair behind her ear.

'What was that?'

'I said, what about Mrs Cassidy? Check out isn't until lunchtime. We can't arrive back before two at the earliest.'

'Don't worry about that. It's all sorted.'

She's frowning at him now. 'But Dan, she's a nice old lady. You said so yourself. We can't interrupt her weekend to ask her to leave early. We broke her vase. She gave us a lovely case of expensive red wine.'

Dan sighs. He's tired, and now stoned. She deserves the truth. Or at least *some* of the truth. His hand rubs the back of his neck as he clears his throat.

'Listen, love, Mrs Cassidy isn't actually staying in your house. Her stepson is.'

'Her stepson?'

'Yep. Hopalong. He's looking after——'

'*"Hopalong?"*' Anna repeats the word, her gaze to the floor, as if she's heard the name before and will find some memory of it at Dan's feet. She looks dazed and brittle, as if this piece of news might be the one to finally break her.

Dan could kill himself for bringing the sicko's name into the space between them.

'So, you've been messaging her stepson, this *"Hopalong"*?' Anna stares at him, panic on her pinched face. 'Dan, the cats. Are the cats okay?'

'Sweetheart, the cats are absolutely fine. You'll see for yourself. We'll be home in a couple of hours. It's all arranged. Nothing to worry about. I'll just finish off here and then we can hit the road, okay? You go and get dressed.'

He's turned to busy himself at the fridge, taking out the bacon and eggs and milk, and shoving them impatiently into the cool box. Anna is hovering, her eyes on him, but he's told her enough. She doesn't need to know the old woman died last year. And she definitely doesn't need to know about the sick video of the cats.

As he shoves the laptop into his bag, he takes another glance at his watch and wills Anna to hurry the hell up. They should be home in two hours. What harm will it do to keep her in the dark a little bit longer?

# TWENTY-ONE

SOMETHING'S UP WITH DAN. He's rushing around like a headless chicken, packing up their things, eager to get home. Inwardly, Anna's livid that he's lied to her about who's been staying in her house. Who the hell is this stepson? And where has Anna heard the name before?

*Hopalong* …

Such a childish nickname. At least Dan confirmed with him that the cats are okay. Anna sighs and rolls her shoulders back. They'll hit the road shortly, but for now she just needs a couple of minutes. Last night's argument chased away any chance of sleep until about four this morning, and now she's shattered. Her throat is itchy and she can feel the start of a head cold coming on. She's looking forward to her own bed later, but for now she just wants to steal a moment to scan the news. She spots her phone, lying abandoned by the fruit bowl. As her fingers wrap around it she remembers Dan's cruel jibes from last night. He actually called her a junkie. Her cheeks flush a little, but she forces her anger to dissipate. They need to put it behind them. She heads for the front door, leaving Dan to finish emptying out the fridge.

'Back in a minute, Dan.'

'Okay, love. I'm nearly done. We'll hit the road in five?'

As Dan turns to look at her, his face falls when he realises Anna's not yet dressed. He glances at his watch, but Anna turns and pulls the door quietly behind herself and steps outside. A ghostly mist has swallowed the morning and seems to ebb and flow in front of her, a living thing, expectant. She leans her bum on the edge of an old wooden seat near the front door and tugs the neck of her dressing gown tight over her chest. It's a bit silly for her to be outside with damp hair and a thin dressing gown when she feels a head cold coming on, but she can't stand Dan looking at her when she's on her phone now.

Under her fingertips the lock screen image on her phone brightens into life. Like every other morning since Ger vanished, Anna makes the sign of the cross on her forehead, closes her eyes momentarily and recites a fleeting silent prayer.

*'Please God, bring her home safe.'*

She looks back at the screen. It's on nine per cent charge.

*Shit.*

Then she notices the four missed calls from Juliette.

*Shit. Shit.*

Anna pushes herself off the bench, hits the redial button, and stares off into the mist as she presses the phone to her ear.

'Anna.'

'Hi Jules. How's things?'

'Anna? Can you hear me?'

'Yes. Yes. Hold on!' Anna moves away from the house, the mist parting, then swallowing her, as she searches for a better signal.

'Jules, can you hear me? I think the weather's stuffing up reception.'

'Just about. It's weak. Listen, Anna, I've been trying you for ages. Did you lose your phone?'

There's something odd in Juliette's tone. A barely suppressed layer of impatient annoyance. But something else too. Something dark. Anna clears her throat, unable to admit that Dan had confiscated her phone last night.

'Sorry, it was on silent all night. Is everything okay?'

'Christ, Anna. Where to start. So, your cat, the ginger one—'

In the background of Juliette's house, a kid has started bawling. Anna presses the phone tighter to her skull, a panicky nausea arising from her belly.

'Juliette? What happened to Nip?'

But her neighbour is momentarily distracted, yelling a threat at her six-year-old twin boys. Anna paces blindly in the mist.

'Sorry, Anna. The boys are playing up. They'd a terrible night's sleep. As did I.'

She pauses, but Anna has no time for games.

'Jules, please. What happened to Nip?'

Although the damp mist washes over every part of her exposed skin, it's a sheen of cold sweat that Anna now wipes from her hand onto her bathrobe. If anything happens to those cats she'd never forgive herself. Everything needs to be exactly as it was for when Ger returns home.

'Oh, the ginger cat's fine. A bit bedraggled is all. It turned up on my doorstep this morning, looking a bit the worse for wear. Wet and cold. Hair stuck up in different directions. But that's not why I was calling you last night.'

'And the black cat? Any sign of Tuck?'

'Put that down!'

Juliette's shouting at her twins again. Anna leans her backside against the car and wills the two kids to settle down.

'Juliette. The black cat?' A tightness has established itself in Anna's jaw and she forces herself to take a slow calming breath. 'What happened last night?'

'Well, as I said, I did try you multiple times.'

'And as I said I'm sorry I missed your calls, Jules. Maybe you should have tried Dan.'

A short incredulous laugh comes down the phone.

'I did try Dan. Several times as well. Obviously you were both otherwise engaged!'

There's a sharpness in her neighbour's tone, and Anna is pulled back to a memory of Dan killing the incoming calls last night while he was trying to surprise her with the holiday. A mate from the building site, he'd said. Someone wanting to go for a farewell beer, he'd told her. Anna closes her eyes and groans.

'I'm sorry Jules. We were both a bit distracted. Why did you ring last night?'

'The racket coming from your place! I nearly called the cops. Maybe I should have.'

'What sort of racket?'

'Loud music. Not your sort. More, I dunno, like angry man music. You know that awful growly satanic shite. At two this morning, Anna!' Juliette has paused and Anna senses she's savouring the drama. 'There was something else.'

'Go on.'

'Well, I couldn't be sure if it was part of the music or not. But at one stage I could have sworn I heard a woman crying, like wailing, you know?'

Anna hasn't yet had breakfast but she can suddenly taste vomit edging up her throat.

An air of remorse filters into Juliette's next words, her voice losing its earlier gusto. 'I regret not ringing the Guards. I just couldn't be a hundred per cent sure if I was hearing things…' Big buxom Juliette sounds beyond ashamed.

'I'm so sorry, Jules. It was actually supposed to be a nice old lady staying at mine, but her stepson is there instead. Dan just informed me. Look, I'm sure it was just the music, or him and a girlfriend in the throes of passion, yeah?' Anna's words echo in the murky stillness and she wonders who she's actually trying to convince. She looks over in the direction of the house, its outline a barely-there smudge in the mist, grateful that Dan is packing. Anna will travel in her nightgown if she has to. She starts back towards the house, eager to get on the road now.

'Jules, we'll leave here in a minute. We'll be home in less than two hours. Leave it with us, okay? He'll be gone this morning.'

'He's already gone.'

'What?' Anna stops just short of the front door.

'I got back from yours a couple of minutes ago. I went over to give him a piece of my mind. You know me, I'm fearless, won't take any shit. As I climbed over the stone wall I only got a brief look at him. A shifty looking fella of about thirty. Dirty fair hair, a bit stocky. Might have been limping. I yelled across to him, but the fecker ignored me, just slammed the door on his shitty white van.'

Anna's hand goes to the door frame to steady herself.

'A white van?'

'A white van, yep. A beaten-up old yoke with dark windows. Next thing I know, his tyres are screeching on your driveway and he's out of there like a speed demon. Frigging nutcase. In a big hurry to get somewhere. I wouldn't be surprised if—'

But Juliette's words are lost. Anna has lowered the phone from her ear and her finger terminates the phone call, instantly thrusting her into an eerie silence. She steps back from the door. She needs a moment.

A snapshot of Ger that final evening, golden in those dying flickers of twilight. The white van pulled up by the pavement, Ger stopping to help a lost stranger. The image has haunted Anna every day since that night in July, and now, as she tilts the phone, her eyes back on the lock screen image, she searches her friend's face for some guidance, some confirmation that she's not going crazy.

*Hopalong*

The name tugs at her attention, and this time Anna's mind is whisked back to yesterday's panicked sprawl on the ground in front of a shack, when the old tramp with the white hair mouthed the name. What was he had said about him?

*He likes them pretty... likes to cut and slice.*

A lump comes to Anna's throat. And she remembers the uncertainty in the old man's eyes, can see now that maybe it wasn't a threat after all, but a warning, a cold fear floating just beneath the surface of his words. There had been a wariness in him, an air of a scrawny dog kicked one too many times by a brutish master.

Anna's mind splinters into a thousand thoughts which then rush back in a roar of white noise, each one screaming to be heard, until one rises above all the others, demanding her attention.

This stranger, this man, who has been staying in Anna's house... is he the one?

She turns to the mist, the world before her devoid of solidity. She shakes her head, tries to dislodge the silly notion, but the question repeats itself.

*Is he the one?*

The words hang in the grey before her. From deep within, she senses the rousing of her old familiars, doubt and paranoia. They circle the question, leap and claw for it, try to snag it and pull it back down where it can lie as broken remnants of fleeting foolishness. There must be a thousand white vans with tinted windows in the country. Yet the simple question lingers with a quiet strength in front of her. And she remembers the shack with its stained mattress. And she imagines the woman's screams that Juliette heard last night. A giddy nausea washes over her. And she knows in her core that she's found him.

Anna cocks her ear. Dan is dropping their bags on the floor just inside the front door. He'll be out in a moment. She'll tell him. Then she'll call the cops and explain her theory to Rooney. She takes another moment and inhales the chill dampness. It begins to sober up the chaos in her mind and reminds her no, she is on her own now. Dan will just laugh at her. And the cops will dismiss her. She's done with being patronised and placated. Ger used to say that the definition of insanity is repeating the same behaviour and expecting a different outcome. Well, no more. Anna slips the phone into her dressing gown pocket and turns for the front door, her fingers uncertain as she raises them to push it, her brain whirring at the idea of what lies ahead. For the first time in a long time, a quickening comes to her pulse and an unsteady, tentative hint of hope manages, barely, to take flight.

# TWENTY-TWO

THE CAR IS PACKED. Anna has dressed hastily, but stands out of sight, just inside the front door. She listens as Dan's hands drum an impatient tattoo on the roof of the car. But she needs another minute. It's all happening too quickly now. His footsteps crunch up the driveway.

'Come on, love. Let's go, yeah?'

He's in the doorway, a distracted scowl on his face as he glances back through the mist to the thorny laneway and their drive home. She's never seen him this antsy, so keen to get on the road. But there's something else, just below his impatience. A barely contained explosive energy. His fists are balled, his brow is furrowed. As he extends his arm to shepherd her outside, Anna avoids eye contact. He'll know something's up if he looks her in the face. Anna never could lie and now the slow wave of tension rolling up her neck begins to clamp her brain. She could vomit.

'I thought we'd be on the road by now.' He's checking his watch again.

When she glances over the top of the car to where he's standing at the driver's door, he seems to catch something in her expression.

'You alright?'

Anna nods but says nothing. If she opens her mouth there's a risk her theory might spill out onto the roof of the car and lie exposed between them in all its batshit craziness. Concern flashes across Dan's face and now he's coming around the car to give her a quick mollifying hug. It's the last thing Anna wants, and she forces herself not to bristle as his arms envelope her. She presses her fingernails into the palm of her hand, the pain momentarily quashing the swell of self-doubt. The past three months have been a marathon, and, if her theory is correct, she's mere metres from the finish line now. She cannot mess this up. She owes it to Ger.

'Shit!' Dan crouches suddenly and Anna follows his gaze.

'You have *got* to be kidding me.' The passenger-side front tyre is flat. Dan rubs two fingers along the rubber then stands abruptly.

'Fuck!' He kicks the side of the tyre with his boot.

He's pacing, rubbing the short hair at the back of his neck again, and muttering to himself. The spare wheel in the boot was never replaced after Anna's last puncture a few years back. Dan's chewing on his bottom lip and looking off down the laneway, just visible through the mist.

'I'll go to the garage. The one we passed on the drive here, past the slaughterhouse.'

'Do you want me to come with you?'

'Nah, you stay put. I'll be faster on my own. I'll run there, grab a replacement wheel, and hopefully whoever's there can drive me back here.'

It's Sunday. They're in the middle of nowhere. There will be no one. Anna says nothing.

He's already limbering up, stretching his quads. A few months ago, Anna bought him a yellow Helly Hansen waterproof jacket, after he'd turned up soaking wet on her doorstep one too many times after being caught in the rain. Now, Anna spots the jacket lying across the back seat by their bags.

'You should bring your jacket, Dan. There's heavy rain on the way.'

'Nah, I'll overheat. It'll just slow me down. You head back into the house, stay warm.'

Anna nods and turns for the house. With her gaze fixed on the front of the Cassidy house, she feels Dan's eyes on her back. And suddenly, without warning, the ground shifts beneath her. She stumbles slightly, then comes to a halt, her skin prickling as a darkness within strains to be heard. If her hunch is correct, if they've been staying in the home of the man who abducted Ger, then... the thought peters out, too overwhelming to finish. Anna swallows, her throat tight, but the notion is insistent and whispers on. And with a chill dread it occurs to Anna that there is no one around to help her, no one to hear her if she screamed her lungs out right now.

'Dan?' Her voice is quiet, uncertain of what she's about to ask, but the words won't be stopped.

'What?'

'Why here?'

'Come again?'

She turns slowly to face him, ignoring the paranoia nipping at her ankles. He's watching her, his eyes guarded.

'Why did we come here? Of all the places we could have come, why this particular house?'

He's frowning, his mouth slightly open, but no words are forthcoming. And as she watches his expression, for the first time she wonders if he's been wearing a mask this whole time. Who is this man standing before her, this man she brought into their lives? Just who is Daniel Pell? A small tremor has started in Anna's left leg and her feet desperately want to move her quickly back into the house where she can slam and lock the door. But she forces herself to stand her ground. The silence between them heaves with wariness. He raises a hand to rub the back of his neck, then shakes his head with a look of tired disgust.

'I'll be an hour. Ninety minutes tops.'

Anna watches him turn and jog off, his back losing definition as he vanishes into the mist. She closes her eyes and listens, thinks she can hear his feet on the loose stones of the lane. But soon she stands in absolute silence, finally alone.

She takes a few urgent steps after him, her chin softening, her eyes beginning to prickle. Is it too late to call after him? To shout his name and cry her apologies into the mist? She stops, tilts her head towards her chest and groans. She's an idiot. She shouldn't be treating Dan like a suspect. He's done nothing wrong. Yet something just doesn't add up. If they've been staying in the home of the man who took Ger... she stops the stupid thought in its tracks, shaking her head at the utter lunacy of such an immense coincidence. She rubs both hands down her face, hoping for a light bulb moment to make sense of it all. Either she's finally lost the plot and this latest theory has loosened her remaining grip on reality. Or else Dan and this Hopalong character are in cahoots. Anna turns for the house. No matter how monumental the coincidence, the main thing is she's fairly certain she's found the guy. That's all that matters right here and now. She kicks the front door shut behind herself. She needs proof and she doesn't have much time.

In the kitchen, she walks straight to the wall-mounted magnetic knife holder. The blades are arranged left to right, from largest to smallest, but the middle knife is missing. Anna's gaze lingers on the gap while her hand drifts around her back and squirrels in between her jacket and jeans. Her fingers wrap snug around the handle of the missing knife. She tilts it to the weak light filtering in through the kitchen window. There is no evidence of rubber from where she leaned in under the car to stab at the tyre. She feels no pang of guilt as she thinks of Dan trekking to the garage. Whatever it takes to buy herself a little more time here. Anna wipes the blade carefully on her jeans, then clicks the knife back into place amongst its siblings on the magnetic strip.

She leans her elbows on the countertop for a moment and tries to calm the swoosh of blood in her skull. She's got all the symptoms of adrenal fatigue, three months of being constantly primed for fight or flight leaving her brain melted, her muscles sore and spent. She knows she could be about to make a terrible mistake and as she stares through the window into the ghostly milkiness beyond, a rising ripple of dread laps at her insides. She cannot afford to be scared or doubtful now.

*Just focus on saving Ger.*

Her hand returns to the knives on the wall, but this time her fingers find the largest blade. She grips it tight and turns — as ready as she'll ever be — and walks out into the cold mist.

# July

# TWENTY-THREE

SOMEONE RAPPED THE LETTERBOX. Anna shuffled forward and pushed herself up stiffly from the armchair. It was probably just Juliette, wondering if there were any updates. Today marked one long and hellish week since Ger vanished and the lack of progress on finding her now twisted like a dagger in Anna's gut. She turned into the front hall and instantly her heart skipped a beat. She could see Ger through the frosted glass of the front door. Anna raced the short distance to the door, sweet relief coursing through her veins. Ger was home. All was right with the world once more.

Anna yanked open the door, a demented expression of pure gratitude taking over her face. But something wasn't quite right with her best friend's features. The cheeks were sunken. The hair was short and slightly brittle. Those familiar eyes had had their colour saturation turned down. The cruel reality slammed into Anna and she had to grip the door frame to stop from collapsing as she waited for her lungs to once again draw in air. There was no concealing her disappointment as she dredged up a smile for Assumpta Kelly. Behind Ger's mother, Phelim, the father, hesitated by the car. He was looking up at the guttering on the front fascia of the house, no doubt preparing to slip into the relative safety of landlord duties.

Anna looked back at Mrs Kelly. They'd spoken every evening since Saturday and had agreed a strategy of the Kellys staying back at the family home in Drogheda in case Ger turned up there, while Anna would remain at home in Skerries for the same reason. But now here they were on Anna's doorstep, unannounced, and Anna's heart shattered at the sad sight of them both. Once feisty Assumpta and burly Phelim, now replaced by a pair of shrunken strangers, each regarding her with a look of abject confusion. Assumpta, always dressed to the nines and with never a hair out of place, had her cardigan on inside out and a rogue dab of lipstick on her upper teeth. Anna leaned in to give her a hug and then stepped back silently to invite them in.

The living room stank of old takeaways. Anna tugged open the curtains and cracked the top window for air, but the daylight only illuminated the squalor she'd been living in for the past days. She knew she probably looked demented and that the house was an absolute pigsty, but now, seeing everything through her visitors' eyes, she felt flustered with embarrassment. She smoothed her mess of hair back off her face and pulled up the zip on her stained hoodie. The coffee table sat crammed with abandoned mugs of tea and half-eaten boxes of pad thai and palak paneer. On the sofa, a dumped laundry basket of damp clothes gave off a musty pong. Anna snatched it up and gestured for Assumpta to sit down, but the woman was flitting from one edge of the room to the other, as if looking for clues, whittling on with a nervous distraction Anna recognised in herself. Ger's dad, Phelim, a towering man, had always made Anna think of Liam Neeson, or some other leading man from Hollywood's golden era. But now he dithered at the sliding door in the kitchen, vacant eyes directed out to the garden beyond, his back to the women, his hands dug deep in his trouser pockets.

Assumpta eventually allowed Anna to guide her over to the sofa, where the woman sat tense, ready to spring into action. She was meant to be in New York, she'd reminded Anna. Last Saturday she'd been only moments away from boarding the plane to JFK for her annual trip to see Lorcan, his wife and the grandkids, when she'd noticed the missed calls from Anna.

'Lucky', she gave a tragic smile to Anna.

'Lucky', she repeated weakly, staring dead-eyed towards the dormant fireplace.

Anna said nothing, just looked to the fireplace too.

'And the police have nothing new to go on?'

'No. No, I'm sorry.' Anna dropped her gaze to the twist of tissue in Assumpta's fingers. She'd been keeping the Kellys in the loop since the previous Saturday when the cold realisation of Ger's vanishing had hit her. But she understood the mother's need to replay it all in person, just like Anna had been rehashing and reliving it all, sifting through her memory, formulating theories a thousand different ways. Over the past sleepless nights, Anna's mind had lurched off in more and more ridiculous directions, searching and failing to find some logical yet harmless explanation. Had Ger been forced to do a runner, and was currently laying low somewhere, biding her time until the coast was clear? Was she a problem gambler who'd racked up huge debts? Or a secret member of some controlling cult and she'd wanted out? Just as soon as Anna would come up with a possible theory, she'd dismiss it in all its silliness again. If Ger had been in any kind of trouble she would have told Anna. Even if she'd felt compelled to disappear for her own safety, she would have found some discreet way to let Anna know. She was the least selfish person in the world and she'd have known only too well how this would be destroying everyone.

'And she definitely never made it home?'

'No. We're pretty sure about that.' Anna took a sip of water from her glass. 'The clothes she was wearing, they're not upstairs. Neither are her phone or bank cards. The neighbours didn't see her. One theory is that she took a shortcut home

147

through the cemetery. But no witnesses have come forward. Nothing's turned up.'

'Jesus, Mary and Joseph.'

Anna focused her eyes on the mottled skin of Assumpta's knuckles. A subtle shaking had set up home in the poor woman's hands. In the background, the sliding door in the kitchen slammed shut in its runner, startling both women.

'For goodness sake, Phelim!' A hand patted Anna's knee. 'I'm sorry about that. Clumsy oaf.'

Anna turned to see Mister Kelly now standing outside, surveying the garden. He walked quickly out of view and Anna turned her attention back to Assumpta, a sudden flash of Ger in her mother's eyes causing Anna to catch her breath.

'Anna, is there anything, *anything*, you haven't told the Guards.' A subtle leaning towards Anna now, a conspiratorial narrowing of the eyes. 'Something you're holding back? Something we should know?' Assumpta's hands reached for one of Anna's, her grip insistent.

Anna pressed her lips together and shook her head. There wasn't. Hand-on-heart she could honestly look Ger's mother in the eye and definitively say, no, there was nothing she was holding back.

Sergeant Rooney had already spoken to the Kellys on the phone earlier in the week. And he'd been back-and-forthing via email with Lorcan in Brooklyn too. His sidekick, Ponytail, had run questions past the book club, and the cops had visited this house too. While looking through Ger's things they'd taken a cursory snoop around the other rooms, including Anna's. *Good*, Anna had thought after they'd left. Herself and Dan would be suspects — Anna wasn't naive — and she was more than fine with that. They'd also checked out the CCTV footage from the pub and had no doubt searched for evidence of some heated argument with Ger. *Good*, she'd thought again. The sooner they exhausted every avenue of suspicion with herself and Dan, the sooner they could scrub them from their list of suspects and focus instead on the driver of that white van. And let's not forget Gavin Sweeney. Had he something to do with it? Anna didn't know, but each time she thought of how he'd treated Ger over the past few months she wanted to destroy the slimy prick.

In the background, the lawn mower kicked into life. Phelim would be cutting the lawn that Dan had done on Tuesday. Anna stood.

'I'll just stick the kettle on and then we can take a nice cuppa out to Phelim, yeah?'

Anna stared at the kitchen tap as the kettle boiled. She'd been averaging no more than three hours sleep since last Saturday and it was suddenly catching up on her. It wasn't like she couldn't skull wine or smoke one of Dan's joints and find a bit of escape that way. She just couldn't face the thought of Ger coming in the door to find her passed out on the sofa, failing as a friend again. No, Anna would be present, through all the forthcoming ups and downs, the shit and pain and whatever else was yet to fall in her lap, she would be ready for it all. She owed that much to Ger.

With the kettle boiled and the tea poured, Anna could hear a barely stifled sobbing coming through from the living room. She gently slid open the back door and carried out a mug of tea and a plate of plain biscuits. The lawn mower was silent again, replaced by the comforting song of finches in the hedgerows. Anna rounded the corner of the house and froze. Mister Kelly was bent over the handle of the Flymo, his strong shoulders quaking silently, his profile contorting itself into the ugliness required to weep. For as long as she'd known him, Phelim Kelly had epitomised everything solid and dependable in the world, his evergreen trust in life buoying Anna more than she'd realised. He'd stood beside her when she'd buried her own father, ready and willing to fill that void. Now it was her turn. She should go over to him, play the daughter role, put a comforting arm around his shoulder and promise him that everything would be okay, even if it mightn't be. But Anna just stood there, awkward and useless, weighing up which weeping parent she should attempt to console. She was spent, no use to anyone. She retreated silently back indoors and tipped Mister Kelly's tea down the kitchen sink.

'Anna?'

'Yes Assumpta. Just coming.'

Assumpta was at the window, her back to Anna, looking out at Juliette from next door walking up the lane with her unruly labs and twin boys. 'I just don't get it.'

Anna settled back into her armchair and exhaled. 'What's that?'

Assumpta turned, eyes damp, arms folded. 'I mean, I just don't get why Geraldine would walk home alone…'

Anna wanted to look away, had a sudden urge to get up and run, but Assumpta was approaching steadily, and now looked down at her, a confused gaze searching Anna's face for answers.

'I know Geraldine's a fully-grown woman and she doesn't need to be chaperoned. But why didn't you just walk home together?'

Anna reached to the coffee table for her glass of water, a need to busy herself. The glass wobbled in her grip and a small trickle ran down her chin.

'Not that I'm implying this was your fault, Anna. Goodness, no. That's the last thought on my mind…'

The Kellys left not long after, but Assumpta's question lingered in the shadowy corners of the house and trailed Anna from room to room. It pulsed and grew as that evening's light faded. Now, Anna stood in the doorway of Ger's bedroom. Above her, the skylight framed a dusky sky, the first faint stars struggling to show themselves. Dan was staying at his own place tonight and apart from the distant barking of one of Juliette's dogs, the house lay silent.

*Why didn't you just walk home together?*

As the loaded question replayed in her mind, a familiar little prickle came to the back of Anna's eyes.

'Because I'm the world's worst friend, Assumpta. Is that what you want me to say?' Anna's words hung harsh in the stillness of the room and she swallowed down the tightness in her throat. They all thought it. The cops, the Kellys, Ger's colleagues, their mates in the village. They all knew the ugly truth. That Anna Moriarty would rather stay out on the piss than be a good mate. Even now she could still see the hurt and disappointment in Ger's eyes as she turned to leave Mulligan's.

*So much for sisters before misters.*

Anna stared at the clothes rail in front of her, dazed and lost for a moment, before raising her fingers to touch the empty hanger at the end. For the hundredth time, she stared at the hanger missing the ivory-coloured halter neck top, a reminder that Ger never made it home that night.

# October

# TWENTY-FOUR

A LONE RAVEN EYEBALLS ANNA as she closes the front door of the Cassidy house. She wonders if it's the same bird that swooped her two days ago at the abattoir. In front of her the trees lean into each other, shrewd and conspiring, whispering and watching to see what she'll do. Around their trunks, the mist still lingers. The raven's black eyes offer Anna nothing but a sly warning of some danger she'd be wise to heed. The bird cocks its head, picking up some sound beyond Anna's range of hearing, then takes sudden flight. The glossy ink of its wingspan draws Anna's eyes until it vanishes in the direction of the thin path coming from the woods. Anna is alone once more. A hard silence hangs all around her and she clears her throat to pierce the stillness. Then, before she can change her mind, she sets off along the path which snakes into the woods.

Above the trees, the slate sky has begun to thicken, more rain on the way. The chill air has brought the fine hairs on her arm to attention. She fixes a strand of loose hair behind her ear and tries to quell the inner voice which is screaming at her to stop, to turn around and just call the cops, that it's not too late. But she can't. That moment has passed, and anyway, the cops would only advise her to stay put, not touch anything, not *do* anything. She can wait no longer.

Anna's feet are unsteady on the uneven ground and she contemplates using her phone torch to cut through the murky shadows stretching between the base of the trees. But she needs what's left of her precious battery. A trickle of sweat runs down her spine as sneaky brambles reach towards her arms. Anna pushes on.

From some deep childhood place of soothing, the first bars of *Greensleeves* arise from her unconscious mind so that she finds herself nervously humming as her feet force her further into the woods. For a delicious moment she gives her thoughts over to ice-cream vans and summer holidays by the beach. Anything to stop her from thinking of what lies ahead.

Something snaps on the ground. Anna freezes like a spooked doe, her grip tightening on the handle of the butcher's knife. Yesterday she was warned to stay away from the shack. But today what choice does she have? A chill courses through Anna's veins, but she does her best to ignore it, instead bringing her focus to the leaf-strewn winding path before her.

*Come on, Anna. Come on.*

Only ten minutes ago she went to the loo back at the house, but already her bladder is begging for her to turn around and go again. Any excuse to stop this madness. She forces her feet to quicken, no time for doubt. She has a job to do. Just the thought of Ger being taken away by some sicko, tortured and made to scream like that woman Juliette mentioned… Anna's stomach churns at the memory of what she saw in the shack yesterday. The camera tripod and the stained mattress. Does this bastard have other shacks? How many girls might be out there right now, their screamed pleas heard only by heartless trees and soulless ravens. To think of Ger chained up, somewhere like this. Anna fights back the threat of nausea. She must be braver than she's ever been.

*Sisters before misters, sisters before misters.*

She panic whispers the sad little mantra to herself, aware how ridiculous it sounds as she walks alone towards God-knows-what. She could kick herself for not leaving a note for Dan. She repeats the words, but they are impotent against the rising fear that now brings a shallowness to each breath.

Soon the thickets of bush and trees begin to thin out, and the narrow path widens into the familiar scrubby open patch Anna stumbled upon yesterday. There it is, the shack with its rust-coloured stains, the ground before it strewn with the broken bottles, breeze blocks and old bricks she scrambled over yesterday. It all sits untouched, as if awaiting her return. An eerie whistling sound plays up through the trees from the lake down below where she first spotted the old man yesterday. Anna stays hidden just out of sight of the shack, silent and observant for a moment. She glances back into the gloom of the woods to confirm she hasn't been followed, then steps carefully onto the scrubby wasteland. Once more she feels observed, eyes watching from the shadows.

Her feet tread cautiously, picking across the blocks and glass. As she approaches the front door she bends down and picks up a piece of broken brick from the rubble-strewn wasteland. The heavy padlock on the door of the shack waits expectantly. She places her knife on the ground, then glances around once more, knowing she'll have to be quick. Anna scrunches her eyes shut and brings the brick down hard against the padlock. The noise echoes through the trees. Anyone nearby will have heard it. Anna opens her eyes, no time to waste, and swallows at the sight of the smashed padlock. She has no excuse now.

*What the hell am I doing?*

She picks up her knife, sucks in a deep breath and creaks open the shack door.

# TWENTY-FIVE

THE SMELL HITS HER LIKE AN OPEN HAND across the face. She gags and blinks as a sour stench forces its way up her nostrils. A bluebottle is buzzing listlessly in the corner near the makeshift kitchen where a bowl on the floor contains something lactic and lumpy. Anna pulls the neck of her top up over her nose and closes the shack door behind her.

*Touch nothing. Just look. Take pictures.*

The inside of the shack is warmer that it should be, the air stifling and stale. Anna places her knife on the windowsill so she can slide off her denim jacket. The sense of evil she felt yesterday looking in through the window is magnified today, no pane of glass to separate her from it. Iron hooks leach rusty stains like bloody teardrops down the wall. The cutting tools all around her seem eager for use. She shouldn't dawdle, but she's struggling to look away from the pained expressions of the dead animals, all missing eyeballs and rictus grins of jagged teeth. Did Hopalong do all the cutting and slicing, she wonders?

Anna forces her attention to the one object in the room that is more unsettling than anything else: the camera tripod. It stands alien in its otherwise organic surrounds, sleek and black and totally at odds with the overall air of decay. The camera is absent, but the tilt of the plate at the top of the central column confirms her suspicions. Whatever was happening on the mattress on the floor was its most recent point of focus.

Anna crouches down closer to the mattress. It is beyond filthy, the ugly purple-brown flowery print faded from wear, and torn in places, but now also covered with a layered spread of old stains in its soiled centre. In some places the overlapping stains darken to near black. Anna stands again and takes out her phone from her back pocket.

*Six per cent charge.*

She nibbles her bottom lip, but she has no choice. The cops will want to see photographic evidence. As quickly as she can she takes pictures of the mattress, the tripod, the pelts and knives, unable to shake the feeling she is standing in the middle of a crime scene. She swipes through the photos, then puts the phone back in her pocket.

What would Sergeant Rooney see if he was here? Would he see a crime scene? As Anna attempts to see things through his eyes, she feels the doubt start to crawl up her spine. Is there enough here to bring a guy in for questioning? A shiny tripod and some dubious stains on a manky mattress, hunting implements and some dead animals that would make a taxidermist blush. It's hardly compelling evidence. Over at the window the bluebottle bounces drowsily, before giving up and landing back on the rim of the bowl on the floor. What if Anna, in her increasing desperation to find Ger, has latched on to some harebrained notion that this Hopalong character is a serial abductor. Is she about to make an absolute fool of herself? An eyeless rabbit grimaces back at Anna from the far corner of the room. She glances one last time at the sad and grubby contents of the little shack, keenly aware that she might just be trespassing into the life of some lonely little man-child.

*Hopalong.*

She repeats the strange name like an incantation under her breath, as if to draw forth the person in whose private space she's standing.

She should go. As she grabs her denim jacket, she takes a quick peek out the grubby window. But as she picks up her knife, she hesitates, her inner voice telling her she's not yet done here.

To the left of the door is the compact side table she noticed yesterday through the grime of the window. A motley crew of glass bottles and jars cram its surface. There's something precise, even trophy-like, in the arrangement, the larger receptacles towards the back of the cluster, the smaller ones closer to where Anna stands. She leans in closer. The glass of each bottle is cloudy with age, either that or just filthy like everything else in here.

On the only square inch of tabletop that is still bare, Anna spies a small, semi-translucent sliver of seashell. She picks it up carefully and watches as the weak mid-morning light plays over its opaque surface. Perhaps it broke off from an oyster shell at some stage, its lustre long gone from years on dry land. She lays it flat on her palm and touches the thinness of its gentle curve, pressing slightly and surprised to find a subtle springiness pushing back against her fingertip. Anna's finger jumps back and a taste of bile rushes up her throat. It isn't a shell. It's a human fingernail. She flicks it into the corner and frantically wipes her hand on the leg of her jeans.

She forces herself to crouch closer to the cluster of bottles and jars. In among the glassware is a ring with a gemstone. It looks fake, like a piece of costume jewellery. Behind it, nearly obscured by a small glass jar, is a lipstick. Anna reaches for it, knowing she shouldn't touch potential evidence, but unable to stop herself. Her fingers uncap it and twist out the ruby shade, a surreal colour in the weak daylight from the window. It's been used. Anna twists it back and recaps it, throwing it back onto the table. She needs to get out of here.

She stands back from the table, feeling sick, needing air and distance. But as she turns to grab the door she feels the earth shift beneath her feet, all doubt rushing from her body.

In an otherwise unremarkable little glass bottle with a stoppered lid is a small piece of fabric. It's a torn piece of silk. Ivory coloured. From Ger's halter neck top.

# TWENTY-SIX

DAN STOPS TO CATCH HIS BREATH and lets the weight of the new wheel lean against his thigh for a moment. His t-shirt clings to a slick film of sweat on his back and he pulls at it uselessly with his left hand. A faint pattering sound draws his attention to the ugly gash down the side of his right hand. His arm is lifted away from his body to keep the blood off his clothes and he watches as his sweat runs down the build-up of grime on his arm and then winces as it stings the deep cut in his flesh. His eyes follow the little spatter trail of claret back in the direction of the garage. He could kill himself for being so clumsy. Anna is not going to be amused.

When he'd arrived at the garage twenty minutes earlier, he'd banged on the front door and hollered around the side of the building on the off chance that someone might actually live there. But his initial hunch had been right: the place was deserted, and being a Sunday morning in the back of beyond it was highly unlikely that anyone would be turning up. He'd gone around the back, taken a quick piss, and had given the rusty roller door a good shake. He climbed up onto an old oil drum and used a rock to smash a high window, but the bloody drum had wobbled, causing Dan to stumble. Not much, but enough for his hand to make quick contact with a nasty shard of glass. Enough of a gash to require a few stitches later. On the workbench he'd left a bloodstained fifty euro note — the only money he'd had on him

160

— then unlocked the front door and let himself out with a replacement wheel in good enough condition.

So now he's rolling the wheel awkwardly with his good hand, avoiding the bumps and potholes as much as possible. It's slow going, taking longer than he'd planned, likely another hour or so before he can corral the stupid thing as far as the turnoff and then up that brambly little dirt track to the house. He glances at his watch and can't help wondering if Hopalong has woken up and read the snarky message yet. With any luck the freak will still be passed out in bed. Dan's itching to beat the crap out of him, but for now he'll just have to make do with a little delayed gratification.

Overhead the clouds have started to layer over each other, a subtle change to the quality of the light, and he remembers another storm is forecast.

*Another bloody storm.*

Christ, he could never live here, not with the constant threat of rain. He gives the tyre another shove and tries to console himself with thoughts of warmer days back in Australia. In four days' time he'll be on the plane. And after last night's debacle he'll be travelling solo. No bad thing, Anna's well and truly lost the plot. He remembers the way she looked at him earlier by the car, how she asked him, *'Why here?'* The woman's a conspiracy loon now. Dan shakes his head and picks up his pace. Well, he's got nothing left to give her now. He'll drive them back to Dublin then make his excuses. After this evening he's done with her. Good riddance.

A couple of hundred metres up ahead on his left he sees the beginning of the sagging chain link fence.

*Cassidys Meats*

He emits a vexed snort as the old shopkeeper's words from yesterday replay in his mind.

*He enjoyed the butchering a bit too much. Sick bastard. Liked to torture the poor animals.*

As Dan gets closer he looks up at the depressing facade of the abandoned abattoir. So this must be where Hopalong learned to wield his knives, to flail and butcher. Sick bastard. For a long moment Dan broods at the sign, an unease darkening his mind, as he thinks of the two cats back home. He bats the concern away and gives the tyre an impatient shove. It catches the edge of a dip in the road and bounces back, bumping into the bloody wound on his hand. He howls and curses and tries to shake the sudden throb away. Not what he needed today. He'll have to swing by A&E this afternoon to get stitched, the next thing on his list after taking care of Hopalong. He smirks to himself as he imagines Hopalong slumped in a hard plastic chair beside him, black and blue and awaiting his own stitches courtesy of Dan. Taking a quick glance back over his shoulder, Dan finds himself praying for some kindly soul to come along and offer him a lift for the last couple of kilometres. But the road has been desolate and not one vehicle has passed him in either direction since he left Anna over an hour ago. He wipes some sweat off his forehead. He's not had any water this morning and last night's red wine is now setting up a dull echo of pain in his temple.

Dan brings the crunching tyre to a sudden, wobbly stop. He can't be certain, but there just might be someone coming. He turns his head and closes his eyes to listen. Sure enough there's the unmistakable sound of an approaching engine. He peers back to where the road bends among the distant hedgerows and bare trees. A vehicle appears around the corner, still a couple of hundred metres away. Dan wipes his clean hand through his hair and turns to fully face the vehicle. He keeps his position in the middle of the road, leans the wheel against one leg and holds up his good hand to signal the driver for help.

*Good*, thinks Dan as the driver gets closer and he gets a clearer view. *There'll be some room for the wheel in the back.*

Dan hides his bloody hand behind his back, not wanting to dissuade the driver. He must be a local, judging by his confident speed on the narrow road. Dan can just about make out the person behind the wheel now. No doubt a farmer. Dan raises his good hand a few inches higher, but the driver still doesn't seem to have spotted him. He's not slowing down. The engine gets louder and now the driver is looking Dan in the eye. He's a thickset man of about thirty, sandy hair, a shadow of stubble. Dan's muscles tense and he swallows hard. The fucker is going to run him down. At the last minute, Dan throws himself out of the path of the speeding van, landing painfully on his right arm, his bloody hand awash with fresh pain.

'What the hell?'

Overhead a thunderous rumble rolls across the slate grey sky. Dan pushes himself up with difficulty using his good hand. He scrambles up from the scrubby roadside, cursing at the idiot driver. But in the few seconds it's taken him to get back on his feet the speeding van has screeched out of sight.

'Far out.'

Dan rubs at the back of his neck, incredulous, as he looks along the deserted road. Another complaint of thunder echoes across the landscape. His blood continues to patter on the broken road surface, a little heavier now from where the wound has been freshly opened by the fall. He rights the wheel awkwardly. Thank God he insisted that Anna wait back at the house. She'll be drinking tea, warm and safe, lost in her silly conspiracy theories.

*Daft woman.*

Dan wipes the sweat off his brow, then gives the wheel a shove.

# TWENTY-SEVEN

ANNA HAS RUN STRAIGHT TO THE upper heights of the quarry. There's probably one call's worth of precious charge left on her mobile and in this weather she can't risk it on a piss-weak signal back down at the house. Once she's done her call, she'll get back down there and wait for Dan. But right now she's feeling twitchy, her mind racing. In her pocket, her fingers wrap around the cool glass of the bottle containing the fabric from Ger's top. She shouldn't have taken it from the crime scene, but to hell with it. Right now she needs something physical to grasp, a protective talisman to ward off doubt and danger and steer her through the churning currents which lie ahead. She can't wait to tell Dan everything, to show him the little bottle, to bring him to the shack, to recount what Juliette said about the white van and the woman's screams. She needs to watch his face reshape itself in front of her very eyes as any stubborn vestiges of uncertainty evaporate. Anna was right all along and after three long months they're all finally going to believe her. A ripple of self-righteousness stiffens her jaw. She was never paranoid. The bastard in the van did exist. And he did take Ger.

She places her knife at her feet, then tugs her denim jacket tighter around herself. The mist has long gone, whipped away by a strengthening wind, and now the smell of ozone hangs in the air. She is pacing back and forth along the ledge over the quarry, looking out to the patchwork of fields in the distance. Thunder grumbles not far off, and a thick welt of pewter cloud looms

164

steadily closer by the second. She pulls out her phone, dials, and presses it to her ear, aware that it's Sunday morning. She can only hope the man picks up.

As she'd run up here, Anna had planned her words so that she's nothing but efficient with the remaining charge on her phone. If Rooney interrupts her she'll tell him to shut up. She needs to be firm. She needs to tell him her location. She'll give him the bare facts, keep the emotion out of her voice. As always, part of her wants to impress the man.

The mattress, the tripod, Ger's top, the white van, the woman's screams. It's more than enough. As the phone rings in Anna's ear, she indulges herself with the smallest amount of hope. There's no evidence that this Hopalong character has killed anyone. He's not behind bars. So Ger might very well be alive. Anna exhales a giddy sigh and tells herself to calm down. She has to stay focused. If they manage to bring Ger home safely, then and only then might Anna allow herself to exhale, might begin to *think* about forgiving herself for being a bad friend.

The phone continues to ring. She pictures Rooney cursing as her name flashes up on his mobile. Her free hand takes out the little glass bottle. She holds it up and turns it, watching the piece of ivory fabric catch the watery daylight.

'Hello…'

'Sergeant Rooney! I need you to listen—'

'… I'm sorry I can't get to the phone right now. But if you'd like to…'

Anna curses, kicks at the scrubby ground as Joe Rooney's voicemail greeting drags on. She takes the opportunity to glance at her phone.

*3%*

'Sergeant Rooney. Joe. It's Anna. Anna Moriarty. I've found him. The guy who abducted Ger. I've located his lair. Evidence of bestiality. Torture.' Anna's shouting her words in rapid fire. 'I found a piece of Ger's clothing too. Well, a cutting. I need police here ASAP.'

Her phone gives its low charge warning. But Anna ignores it, focusing on giving her location, a rush of words.

'… Cassidy's meatworks. Further along that road is a right-hand turn. About half a kilometre up that single lane track is the house. Hurry. Please.'

She hangs up and prays the Sergeant checks his phone soon. They'll be hours getting here. But they might be able to send a local car, a couple of Gardaí to at least seal off the shack with crime scene tape and start collecting evidence. Anna shields her eyes as a sheet of lightning blinds the land. She turns and squints, her eyes fixed on a point in the distance, where she thinks she can see a glimpse of the long brambly lane way that leads up to the house.

'Come on, Dan,' she whispers into the wind. 'Come on.'

Fat drops of cold rain suddenly explode around her. Down below in the quarry the muddy pools fire off sparks of water. Anna cups a hand over her eyes and looks down towards the lane way again, but it's already lost, obscured by a curtain of rain. A fresh blast of sideways rain catches her in the face and she turns again to face the quarry. She's drenched in seconds, too late to seek shelter now. Then she hears it, through the thunder, the muffled sound of her phone ringing in her inside jacket pocket.

'Anna?'

'Sergeant Rooney. Joe.'

'Anna? Can you hear me?'

Anna pushes the phone tight to her ear and turns her body away from the blasting rain. She hasn't time for one of those frustrating phone calls.

'Joe. Listen to me. Did you listen to my message?'

'I haven't yet, no. Anna, I need you to listen—'

'No, I need *you* to listen. To my message. Immediately.'

She's shouting over the wind and rain. She sounds demented but she doesn't give a damn. In her ear the phone emits another low-charge warning. But the man is blathering on.

'Anna, we need you to come to the station immediately.'

Anna could scream. What is wrong with the fool? She turns, beyond frustrated, and thinks she spots Dan's faint outline in the distance, down on the road. She squints into the rain for a moment. Yes, he's down there, out searching for her with a torch.

'Dan!' She shouts and waves her free hand frantically. She can't see him clearly through the rain but she can see the low beam of his torch stop sweeping the ground and point in her direction. He's spotted her. Anna allows herself to relax a fraction, but the cop is still talking.

'Is Dan with you, Anna?'

'Yes, yes, he's here, go on.'

Dan is about one hundred metres away. Anna watches the beam of the torch as he steadily approaches via a scrubby path Anna wasn't aware of. There's something hypnotic in the gentle rise and dip of the beam. Anna's teeth have begun to chatter, whether from cold or nervous energy, she doesn't know. In the background Joe Rooney is wasting precious time considering his next words. Anna could scream.

'Anna, we've found—'

His words are lost, the phone in Anna's hand buzzing in a death rattle. She stares at it for a long moment, then turns to face the quarry once more, her gaze on the splints and bellows of lightning in the churning mess over the fields in the distance. She screams her frustration into the wind until her lungs are empty. Any remnants of daylight have been leached away by the thick blanket of cloud overhead. It might as well be nighttime. But her annoyance with Rooney has already started to weaken. Everything might just be okay now. Dan is here. Rooney will listen to her message. With any luck a squad car will be on its

167

way over in the next while. She just needs to be patient a little longer. Herself and Dan can dry off down at the house, get warm and wait for the cops. She sucks in a slow breath and forces her shoulders to soften under her wet jacket.

Lightning flashes once more over the fields and as Anna watches the sky she feels a pang of guilt about how she left things with Dan earlier. She shouldn't have directed her paranoia at him. He couldn't have known Ger's abductor lived here, could he? She sighs away the stupidity and rearranges her features into something she hopes resembles an expression of contrition, then turns to watch him approach. He's nearly here, twenty metres or so away, his body still hidden behind the beam of torchlight which dances over the dark scrubby rise. What she's about to tell him is going to knock him sideways.

Anna slips the dead phone back into her jacket pocket and presses the heels of both hands against her closed eyes. A wave of exhaustion washes over her and she's surprised to find hot tears among the raindrops. It must just be utter relief that the end might be in sight, that, please God, they're going to find Ger. The ghost of the dancing torch beam plays across Anna's closed eyelids, its rise and fall uneven. And in that moment, amid the chaos of the storm, a niggling little disquiet in the back of Anna's mind begs to be heard. With her eyes still closed, Anna swallows. Dan didn't pack a torch. And the man in front of her is limping.

She can't move. Her breath is held, her limbs are rigid. She is frozen, a trapped animal in its final moments as the reality hits her. And just then, every fibre of her core screams at her to run. She darts to the left, narrowly missing the edge of the drop, and glances back at the approaching man, a man she's never seen before. The stranger is only metres from her now. A twisted smile clings to his slack face, the look of a hunter who's done this a million times before. And Anna runs for her life.

# TWENTY-EIGHT

ANNA SKIDS AND STUMBLES IN A FLURRY OF TERROR. She hurtles along the edge of the quarry, but he's close behind her, the beam of his torch hitting rocks and grass just in front of her. Ahead, the ledge starts to descend towards the huddle of huge boulders which stand sentry in a spread of murky puddles. Anna's heart pounds and she tastes blood, metallic on her gums. The primeval scene down below her is a desolate place where the cops won't find a dead body for ages. Her foot slides on a narrow shuck of mud and she lands heavily on her backside. But she pushes herself, up and off, scrambling like a wounded animal, speeding down into the quarry as adrenaline spikes her veins.

She reaches the flat base of the quarry and only now does she risk a look back towards him. He's still a few metres above her, on the narrow path down to the base, his bad leg slowing him. A flash of sheet lightning illuminates him momentarily. He's stocky but strong, early thirties but gone to seed. There's a slackness to his unshaven face and the rain has slicked his thinning hair to his scalp. They lock eyes and Anna has a sudden urge to vomit. This is the monster who took Ger. He's shouting down to her, but his words are lost to the pelting rain. He shakes his head in frustration and cups his hand to his mouth, tries again, slowly coming further down towards her with his lopsided gait. But Anna won't be fooled. If she's to be his next victim he can damn well work for it.

She turns her back on him and quickly scans her surroundings. The base of the quarry must be no more than one hundred metres across. Ahead, slightly to her right, is a cluster of granite boulders. She lurches off towards the largest rocks, the mud sucking at her running shoes, her progress painful. How ironic, she thinks, as she pushes on, wild-eyed: all those hours spent pounding the pavement in her running shoes in Skerries so she'd be prepared for this very eventuality, and here she is about to faceplant in mud. For a silly moment she contemplates screaming her lungs out. But what good would it do her? The squally wind fires blinding rain in every direction and plasters her hair to her face.

She skids in behind a large boulder and gasps in air. She pushes her back against the rocky surface. It's taller than a man and it might buy her a moment until he finds her. But she can't hide for long. She sucks in more precious breaths, preparing to move as fast as she can in the mire. Her gut churns as she pictures the knife, sitting uselessly up on the ridge where she left it. How bloody stupid of her. She didn't even leave a note for Dan. She reaches down to the mucky ground to pick up a rock, but what her fingers find is part of something bigger. It won't budge. Anna stands up again, fresh tears stinging her eyes, and feels another yearning to scream out her frustration.

Today will be the day she dies. Down here, alone, at the hands of this monster. To think she was so close to finding out what became of Ger. But now she's fallen at the last hurdle. The man is yelling and cursing, getting closer. Anna closes her eyes and tries to still her pounding heart. Her only hope is that Joe Rooney listens to her message and catches Hopalong in the coming days. Because maybe then there is hope for Ger. Anna will cling to this hope as death takes her.

*I'm so sorry, Ger.*

The beam of the torch sweeps the mud and puddles mere metres in front of her. Anna holds her breath and presses her spine tighter against the boulder. A sound pierces the howling wind. The man is making a whistling noise, eerie in its playfulness, like he's signalling a sheepdog. Anna's bowels spasm. Her hand instinctively reaches for her phone in her jacket pocket, something familiar and solid to comfort her. But the screen is dead in her hand, raindrops beading where Ger's image should be.

'Stupid bitch. Should have minded your own business.'

He's so close now. A hot trickle runs down Anna's thigh and spreads through the denim on her leg. A feverish whisper comes to her lips, a plea to whichever God is listening to give her a quick death.

He's muttering to himself now, his breathing laboured, his voice so close she can't believe he's not yet visible. But the end of his torch is in Anna's periphery. She turns her head cautiously. Momentary silence. The torch is still. And now, with a chill dread, she realises what he's done: he's placed the torch on a rock to fool her, and has crept around the boulder, preparing to grab her from the other side.

Anna squeezes her eyes shut and waits for his calloused hand to grab her throat. Her breath is held. But a moment passes and she hears him again. He's still by the torch, dangerously close. Anna opens her eyes and now she can see his balding pate. She risks inching forward, careful not to make a sound. He's bent over, struggling with his leg. Water has breached the upper limit of his wellie boot. As he pulls at his waterlogged boot, Anna realises it's now or never. She has no choice if she wants to survive.

She grips her phone along its length and raises it above her head. The stocky man bending down in front of her is momentarily vulnerable, exposed, unaware. The bastard is hers for the taking.

Anna hesitates and the moment stretches. If her blow kills him they may never find Ger. Her slick fingers grip tighter on the phone and her eyes fix on a tender-looking spot on the back of his skull. She just needs to knock him unconscious. Anna holds her breath and time resumes.

He looks up as Anna slashes downward with the phone. It misses its target, bouncing off his right temple. He stands upright, temporarily stunned. The skin on the side of his forehead has split and for a moment no blood appears. But when he raises his right hand to the wound a deep gush of crimson swells, then trickles down his face. Anna feels the colour drain from her own face. The man before her no longer looks stunned. He now regards her with a cold fury. Anna drops the phone and stumbles backward, her hand trailing the rough surface of the boulder. She wants to say something, to explain why she did it, but her voice has deserted her, only a nonsense whimper escaping her lips. He lunges and before she knows it she's on the ground. His open hand slaps her once, hard across the cheekbone. Her face stings. Muddy water runs down her collar, her hips and back are soaked in seconds.

'You stupid bitch!'

His hot breath breaks over her face, a stench of stale beer and garlic. Anna's eyes are focused on something gristly stuck between two of his lower incisors. From this angle his slack face sags towards her and Anna lashes out with her hands to scratch it. Even amidst the panic coursing through her veins, she knows to get his DNA under her fingernails. But he jolts his face just out of reach, too quick for her, primed for such moves. His rough hand grips her neck and forces her head deeper into the mire so that Anna's ears fill with water. He shifts to straddle her, one thick thigh on either side of her torso. Anna's eyes strain against the

172

driving rain to properly see him. She is terrified in this moment, but she will force herself to look this monster in his coal-black eyes. His vice-like grip tightens on her throat.

'What do you want from me?' He's snarling through nicotine-stained teeth, his words muffled by the water filling Anna's ears. Her mouth opens and closes, a dying fish out of water.

He adjusts himself above her and hot blood from his open wound drips across Anna's face. The sky above him flashes again and Anna starts to flail. Her hand sweeps frantically through the mud searching for a loose rock or her dropped phone, anything to hit him. But she finds nothing.

'What do you want?' he hisses again, closer to her face.

Anna's vision starts to swim, her world collapsing in at speed. Death is imminent. Her heart pounds, her lungs scream, a final fight for survival from the primordial depths. But she knows it's futile and her feet cease their kicking at the mud. The tension begins to ebb out of her body and the blackness starts to take her down.

The man's body jerks, stiffens, then collapses forward. His torso lands across Anna, his gut pushing against her face. She only manages a shallow sip of air before her mouth and nose fill with water, his weight sinking her further into the murk. She is drowning.

A shift occurs above Anna. Someone is struggling the bulk of Hopalong off to the side. And now a hand grabs the collar of Anna's jacket and pulls her upper body up out of the mud. She coughs out brown water and instinctively sucks greedily at the air. The mystery hand leans her back against the boulder and Anna's body complies, a rag doll without thought or fear, her only intention to beg air into her burning lungs.

'I warned you.'

Anna knows the voice. She forces open her eyes, enough to recognise the stained suit trousers, belted with a piece of twine, now trailing in the mud. She forces her head back against the boulder and blinks up at him through the rain.

The old man from the caravan on the lane way is swivelling his index finger against his temple. His white hair seems to glisten like a dull halo in the rain as he looks down at Anna, then over to the heavyset man heaped face-down in the muck. A worry seems to dawn on his craggy face and a small rock drops from his veiny old hand. Already the blood on its surface is vanishing in the rain.

'Not right.' He says to himself, as he wipes his hands on his stained trousers. 'Not right in the head, at all.'

# TWENTY-NINE

IT'S THE BLUE LIGHT DANCING along the top of the hedgerow which stops him in rigid confusion for a split second. Then he's sprinting, the tyre abandoned, his squelching shoes powering him up the thorny lane way towards the Cassidy house. The scene which quickly unfolds in front of him is surreal. A cop car, a paramedic's van, a white van that he's seen somewhere before. All parked haphazardly in the tightness of the small driveway. The blue light of the cop car continues to pulse over the near landscape. There is no siren. Nothing to have warned him when he was back on the main road.

Dan's chest is tight, an eruption of cold sweat under his rain-soaked clothes. His eyes dart around, but he cannot see her.

*Christ.*

It takes a moment to register the young male cop approaching him. He's talking to Dan, but the words aren't connecting, and as Dan peers over the man's shoulder, his eyes wild, it now clicks. That's the white van that drove him off the road this afternoon. He stares at it, a deep frown creasing his brow, ignoring the policeman in front of him as he waits for this all to make sense. Something in his subconscious draws his gaze away from the van, brings his focus to the cop car. Someone's in there. It takes a moment for Dan's eyes to cut out the flashing blue and settle on the figure watching him from the back seat. His eyes lock on the man who attempted to run him down. The man stares out at Dan, something simmering and inscrutable in his expression, his dark eyes unblinking. He's been in an accident of some sort. A white bandage has been taped to the side of his forehead. A rusty blot of blood has seeped through.

*What the hell happened here?*

'Sir, you'll have to wait back here.'

Dan hasn't realised that he's been trying to push beyond the cop's outstretched arm.

'Where is she? Where's Anna?'

His eyes make another rapid scan of the scene. Someone's lurking in the shadows at the corner of the house, a tatty old man with thick white hair, Dan's seen him somewhere before. He's casting awkward glances over his shoulder, obviously itching to leave, but not yet free to go. The old man holds little interest for Dan right now as his eyes continue to sweep the scene. Then he spots her. A wave of relief almost brings him crashing to his knees. Anna is perched on the back ledge of the paramedic's van, a heavy red blanket draped over her shoulders.

'Anna! Anna! Over here.'

The medic examining Anna's throat now turns and spots Dan, her glance wary, before she returns her full focus to Anna. Dan tries to jostle past the cop once more, but the man keeps his arms held out.

'Sir, if you just step over this way, I need to ask you a few questions.'

'I know her,' Dan tries, before yelling over the cop's shoulder 'Anna! Anna! Are you alright?'

Anna looks up then, startled, lost. Had they sedated her? Dan's never seen her so out of it. The cop's hand is on Dan's upper arm. It's only now that he knows Anna is safe, Dan takes a proper look at the young cop in front of him. He couldn't be more than twenty-five, has probably never had to contend with more than a burglary or a pissed driver. He's taking in the bloody mess of Dan's hand, his eyes trying to ascertain if the blood is Dan's or someone else's. He corrals Dan over to the side of the house, Dan's neck craned to keep an eye on Anna, the cop ensuring good distance is maintained between Dan and Anna, between Dan and the man in the back of the cop car.

'Who is that man? What did he do to Anna?'

'Your name, please.'

'What? Oh for Christ's sake. I'm Daniel Pell. I'm her partner. You can check with her.'

The cop is making minuscule notes in a black notepad he's extracted from his belt.

'Far out, mate. Can you just tell me who the hell he is?'

'It would appear he lives here. This address is on his driver's licence. Anthony Cassidy.'

'He lives here? Anthony...?' Dan stares at the rain-slicked ground. The owner of this place nearly knocked him down earlier in his rush to get here. The same man did something to Anna. Dan swallows as the sickening reality rushes up to meet him. This is Hopalong, the sicko freak who sent the cat video, the guy who Dan baited with a snarky message earlier. In front of him, the cop's shoes are muddy. Dan stares at them as his thoughts solidify. This is all his own fault. He pissed off the guy and then he left Anna to face him on her own. He blows out a long, steadying breath and wonders if he's going to puke over the cop's feet. 'What did he do to her?' There's a coolness to his voice as he meets the Guard's eyes. 'Did he...'

The cop clears his throat. 'I've spoken to them both. Anna struck first. Got him with her phone. Then Cassidy retaliated. It got nasty. He mentioned you sent him a threatening message earlier, something about you going somewhere on his property you shouldn't? That's the reason he rushed back. He said—'

The blood rushes to Dan's head. 'Now just hold on a minute. I unlocked a bloody door in the kitchen, nothing else! That sick bastard sent me—'

But the cop holds up a placating hand, turns slightly. 'You can report it all tomorrow. They'll want to see you up at...' He flicks back a page in the notebook. '... at Skerries tomorrow morning. Sergeant Rooney, is it?

'Are you trying to tell me that psycho attacked Anna all because of a stupid message I sent him? Are you for real?' Dan is rubbing the back of his head with his uninjured hand, and paces like a caged tiger about to strike.

'All I know is that he said something about you trespassing. He wanted to know what youse were up to, seemed to think ye were attempting blackmail. Anna hit him and then he tried to defend himself. It escalated pretty quickly until John-Joe over there stepped in.' The cop gestures with his chin over in the direction of the scruffy old man with the shock of white hair. 'When I pressed Cassidy on what he meant about blackmail, that's when he went quiet. Demanded a solicitor before he'll say another word.' The cop exhales, his breath visible in the dropping temperature. 'Anna mentioned something about a shack—'

'A shack?'

'She wasn't making much sense to be honest. But it's too dark now to go exploring. I'll be back in the morning with another couple of lads. We may need a warrant. Are you heading home today?'

'You mean we can go?'

'After a few more questions. But I reckon the sooner you hit the road, the better...' The Guard glances to the scowling man in the back of the cop car. 'All things considered.'

He jots down some more notes in tiny cursive before he allows Dan to approach Anna. She's still perched on the back of the paramedic's van, her head tipped, wet hair draped forward. As he nears her, the paramedic gives him a tentative smile and offers to tend to his gashed hand. The words seem to jolt Anna out of her stupor. She looks up, a spooked animal, then lunges for

Dan, collapsing against him, blubbering into his shoulder. He's never seen her this bad, not once in the past three months. He hates himself for what he's done to her. He gently forces her back from his shoulder for a moment, his eyes roving her face. She has the air of a mad woman. Her hair is caked in mud and her neck is a bloom of angry bruises. Dan pulls her into an embrace again, unable to look at her. She's babbling on, some nonsense about slashing tyres and a phone call from Juliette, is insisting that they've found the guy. But Dan just cups the back of her damp scalp and tries to shush her. Her words drift past him, towards the trees and into the shadows. Nothing is hitting home. He's brought this on himself. A low boil of rage bubbles within him, needing release, threatening to spill over any second. He stands mute, uselessly trying to calm her, trying to calm himself. They stand in their embrace amid the blue flashing lights, a pair of lovers in a silent dance. He'll push it all deep, deep down to that darker part of himself. But for now, something else has begun to compete with the hot fury inside. A surge of self-loathing, sharp as caustic bile, is sloshing through his veins. He closes his eyes tight. He's failed her as a man.

Soon, the scant daylight is almost depleted from the landscape around them. With his hand bandaged and Anna somewhat calmer, Dan works with the young cop to retrieve and fit the replacement tyre. It's only after Dan has folded Anna carefully into the passenger seat that he feels that pair of eyes on him again. He looks over the roof of Anna's Fiesta to the man handcuffed in the back of the cop car. The young Guard has his back to Dan and in that moment something bestial compels Dan, a switch flicking in his brain. He moves quickly, quietly, hellbent on punching the living daylights out of the fucker. His blood surges, his jaw clenches. With every step he keeps his eyes locked on the cold impassive gaze of this total prick who hurt his woman. The back door of the car is closed. Dan grabs the handle with his bandaged hand.

'Whoah! Get back!'

The cop has spun, momentarily startled, one hand pushing Dan back by the shoulder, his other reflexively moving to the baton at his belt.

'You're a dog, Cassidy! This isn't over!'

Dan's feet skid on a patch of muddy grass as the Guard shoves him back.

'Go home, Dan.' The cop motions to Anna with his chin. 'She needs you. Go on now.'

The beady eyes continue to stare at Dan. It takes every ounce of resolve to break eye contact, to glance at the cop and nod his understanding, before turning and marching back to the car, his heart drumming, his rib cage tight. Dan starts the Fiesta and keeps his eyes on the brambly lane way as he moves them off. They sit in silence for a few minutes, Dan trying to calm his shallow breaths, Anna's head turned to the passenger window. He cranks up the heat as he turns the car out of the lane and onto the main road, keen to leave this nightmare behind them. The uneven tarmac is still glossy with rain, his little trail of blood long washed away. His hand tightens on the steering wheel as they pass the old abattoir with the *'Cassidy's Meats'* sign.

'You didn't know him, did you?'

The question startles Dan. He glances across to find Anna looking at him, her eyes penetrating, frightened, hopeful. Even in the dimness of the inside of the car, he can see the welt of bruises on her neck. They appear to be darkening by the minute. He expects to feel a flush of anger, a pained resentment at her question. But none appears. Her eyes are still on him. He'll forgive her question. After what she's just been through he can hold nothing against her. He places his good hand on her leg.

'Why are you asking me that?'

She's turned to look straight ahead now, her next words low but determined. 'I'm sorry, but I need to ask, I need to hear you say it. That man, he took Ger, Dan. He's hurt other women too. Of all the thousands and thousands of places you could have arranged for us to stay this weekend... It's just beyond coincidental.' Her voice begins to waver. 'I need to know you weren't in on this. That you and him... tell me you don't know him, Dan. Please.'

Dan watches the tremble in her lower lip. Her paranoia has now reached new depths and he hasn't the skills or the energy to navigate her through this. This is a job for the professionals. He won't argue with her, not with only a handful of days to go before he leaves her life for good. She's broken.

'No, love. I didn't know him. I've never seen him before now. I promise.'

Her eyes are back on him. See watches his face for a beat, then turns once more to face the empty road ahead, a slackening coming over her body as she exhales.

'I'm sorry. I just needed to hear you say it.' Her voice is barely audible, her energy spent.

'It's okay, Banana.' He squeezes her leg gently, then returns his hand to the wheel. 'Close your eyes. I'll wake you up when we're home.'

Her head is already tipped back against the headrest, her eyes closed, her next words a whisper as she begins to drop into an exhausted slumber. 'We got the bastard,' she sighs into the darkness. 'We got him.'

# THIRTY

WHEN THEY PULL UP OUTSIDE ANNA'S HOUSE, Dan kills the engine and rubs a tired hand down his face. The motion sensor light that Anna had recently installed near the front door has turned on. God only knows what he's about to discover on the other side of that front door. He exhales slowly, then glances across to confirm that Anna's still asleep. He needs to go into the house alone. She's still slumped in the passenger seat, but her hair has moved during the journey and now Dan can see Cassidy's thumbprints on the pale skin of her neck. He urgently needs to punch something, but as his fingers instinctively attempt to curl, the new bandage, snug and itchy, prevents him forming a fist. He opens the car door, slides out, then closes it softly again, the only sound the soothing ticks of the car engine as it cools.

He enters the house and carefully closes over the front door, standing for a moment, primed and alert. Behind him, the motion sensor light flicks off and he lets the evening gloom of the hallway envelop him. He inhales. Cigarette smoke hits him first, then beyond that, something musky, a stranger's scent. Something else hangs on the air too, perfumed and synthetic. He's had a woman here. At the end of the front hall a pair of low reflective saucers are trained on him.

'Here, puss puss.'

Dan flicks on the hall lamp and crouches down, but whichever cat was there has darted away, no longer willing to trust a human.

He walks cautiously through the house, flicking on each light with a pang of dread in his stomach. In the living room the sofa has been pushed back against the wall. There's spilt beer and something else sticky on the carpet. Empty bottles have rolled or been kicked out of the way, and greasy palm prints cloud the glass of the coffee table where a plate overflows with spent cigarette butts. A thin dusting of white powder streaks the glass surface. Dan wipes a fingertip across the table and rubs the powder across his upper gums.

He reminds himself he doesn't have long, and slides open the patio door to pull in some fresh air. He bounds up the stairs to Anna's bedroom, stopping abruptly when he sees the state of it. Her antique glass lamp is on its side, smashed. The sheets are filthy, and an empty bottle of bourbon lies on the rug. Dan strips the bed and bounds back down to the kitchen where he casts the bundle of sheets and pillowcases into the washing machine. He pours in some bleach for good measure, then slams the door on the machine and cranks on a hot wash.

He works quickly. Within five minutes he's filled a bin liner with bottles, fag ends and a crushed-up pizza box. He's moved all the furniture back where it belongs and has given the bathroom a quick going over. Now he lights a couple of scented candles, then kills all the ceiling lights. Lamps and candles are better in case he's missed anything obvious. The ginger cat has come out of hiding and is wolfing down a can of food he's spooned into her bowl on the slate floor of the kitchen. There is no sign of the black cat yet. Dan stands by the sliding door and taps the top of a fresh can of cat food with the back of a teaspoon, the way he's seen Anna and Ger do a thousand times.

'Here puss puss! Tuck? Tuck tuck.'

The ginger cat has finished her food and is now twirling herself around Dan's ankles, her eyes on the full can, mewling up for a second course.

'Go away, Nip.'

Dan pushes the cat away with his foot, then looks out into the darkness of the back garden again.

*Fuck.*

He turns and heads back up the stairs. If he runs a bath for Anna it might buy him some time. He starts to fill the tub and pours in some bath salts, then heads downstairs. One final glance up the hallway. It's time to get her in. He's at the front door, his hand raised to the latch, when he pauses. He turns for the stairs and a moment later stops at Ger's bedroom door. Thank God, Anna had insisted on locking it before they headed off on Friday afternoon.

'Hello?'

Anna's voice is raspy, barely making it up to Dan from the front hall.

'I'll be down now, love.'

Dan hesitates at Ger's room a moment longer. Once more, he remembers the bruises on Anna's neck. He pictures the dark-eyed menace shamelessly scowling at him from the back of the cop car earlier. The scumbag can rot in hell. From what Dan overheard this afternoon, the Gardaí might just have enough evidence to lock up Cassidy for a long time. Dan glances over the banister. Anna has found the black cat and is nuzzling her face into its fur. The ginger cat has twined her tail around Anna's left leg. Dan exhales. Anna is safe. The house is fine. The cats are alive. And on Thursday morning he will be homeward bound. For the first time in three months he feels his shoulder begin to relax. It's all going to be okay.

# THIRTY-ONE

ANNA'S BEEN AWAKE FOR HOURS. When Dan put her to bed last night she was unconscious before her head hit the pillow, a dreamless sleep, her brain and body utterly spent. But since just after five this morning she's been sitting at her own kitchen table, watching through the sliding door as a shaft of watery daylight stretches slowly across the back garden. The two cats fight for space on her lap and Anna pats them distractedly, seeking a sense of calm in their warm fur. But her fingers can do nothing but fiddle, her hands rearrange everything within reach. In front of her sits another mug of barely touched tea, her third or fourth that morning. She dare not touch coffee. She turns the mug with a jittery hand and looks up at the kitchen clock above the sink. The minutes drag. The Garda Station doesn't open until ten.

When she's eventually able to leave her house she senses a stirring of giddy helplessness. This time yesterday she had nearly given up hope. But now everything's changed, and she's going to have to prepare herself for whatever the cops find in the coming days. She'll give the Gardaí everything she has, but in reality she'll now have to let them do their job, to trust them to step up and prove themselves to be competent.

Anna turns up Strand Street. It's a blustery Monday morning and thin clouds scud overhead. A sea breeze buffets the long woollen skirts of the schoolgirls milling around the bus stop. Today happens to be Ger's birthday and as Anna ploughs down the street, the front of the Garda Station coming into view, she sighs at the spectacularly bad timing of the day. Mister and Missus Kelly are coming down later. They'd planned it with Anna weeks ago, the idea being to have a birthday cake and a flask of tea on the bench at the North Strand this afternoon, just the three of them, to keep Ger in their hearts and minds. But it's the last thing Anna needs right now. She needs practical, not abstract.

As she dodges out of the way of a dog on a leash, she almost barrels into Gavin Sweeney. The guy's face pales as he stumbles out of her path. Anna feels a brief flare of guilt. Even though he was a complete dick to Ger, at least now she knows he didn't have anything to do with her disappearance. She gives him a cool nod, as good as it will get for him today, her focus narrowed as she turns up the neat front path of the village police station. As she enters through the familiar blue door, she finds Ponytail hunched over the computer by the front desk, the desk phone cradled between her shoulder and ear. Anna is surprised to feel a pang of fondness towards her. *Liz*, that's her name. The young woman can't be more than twenty-three or so, and Anna fights the temptation to tell her not to slouch or she'll pay for it later. She's wrapping up the call, a look of concern on her face, as she hangs up.

'Good morning,' Anna croaks.

'Oh, Anna. Hello.' The woman appears startled, uncomfortable even. Perhaps it's the state of Anna's face. She hesitates for a moment. 'I think Sarge is expecting you. One tic.'

She disappears off behind the mirrored glass, leaving Anna to shrug off her jacket and unwind her scarf. Anna wants Rooney to see the woeful state of her neck. She spent a few minutes in front of the bathroom mirror this morning, tentatively touching the bruises with her fingertips, twisting herself in the mirror to see the colours change. She realises she wants the man to

186

acknowledge her as someone who will do what it takes to bring a monster to justice. It frustrates her that she craves his admiration.

Anna paces the length of the counter. A quiet adrenaline has killed off any earlier sleepiness and she now feels more alive than she's felt in months. The door opens behind her and a couple of senior looking cops come in, their expressions impassive. They ignore Anna and head out through the counter and beyond the partition. She hopes they're here to question Cassidy. Every moment counts now. She stops at the community noticeboard and removes and replaces a bent drawing pin. She's trying not to get her hopes up too much, but today's the day this might just come to a conclusion. Ger might be coming home.

'Anna.'

Joe Rooney looks more tired than normal, his eyes regarding Anna with something she can't quite put her finger on. She wonders if he's pissed off she went rogue yesterday, not waiting on the cops to arrive at the Cassidy house before she went head-to-head with Hopalong.

'Come through.'

He's lifted up the hinged hatch in the counter and guides Anna in, wincing as he notices the mess of colour on her neck. She enjoys the warmth of vindication.

*You see*, she wants to shout at him. *I didn't imagine it.*

'Two teas please, Liz' he whispers across to his colleague, as he gestures Anna to the empty seat at his messy desk behind the partition. The other cops have disappeared further out the back. She can hear phones ringing and the low hum of voices.

'So.'

They both sit. He leans back in his chair and rests his hands across his little paunch. His eyes are back on her neck now and he sits up straighter for a closer look.

'The bastard.'

'Understatement of the year, Sergeant.' Anna's raspy voice sounds to her like that of a stranger.

'Are you...'

Anna wafts away his concern. 'I'm fine, seriously.'

'Right. Well, thank goodness. So, is Dan not with you?'

'No, he's finishing up at work.'

'Right.' The cop picks up his pen and puts it down again. Anna guesses it's about now he would usually have had his first cigarette of the day. 'Finishing up?'

'Well, he's flying back to Australia on Thursday, so he's got a lot of loose ends to tie up.' The cop stares at Anna, a million micro-expressions passing over his face. 'Did you not know? His visa expires this coming weekend. He's cutting it fine, as it is.'

'No, I didn't know.' The pen is picked up again. This time a small illegible scribble is made on a virgin page.

'Well, anyway. I'm sure he'd be more than happy to come in if you need him to. Although I don't see why you would.' Anna shifts in her seat. She can feel the man's low energy sapping her own spirits.

'So, has he spoken yet?'

'You mean Anthony Cassidy?'

'Anthony?'

'Yep, Anthony. Or Anto, as he prefers. The Hopalong nickname he picked up at the abattoir was something they never dared call him to his face.'

'Right. So, what have you found out?' There's a no-nonsense briskness to Anna's voice. She can still feel the phantom grip of Cassidy on her neck and it hurts her to speak. But Joe Rooney is pausing and Anna has an urge to reach across the desk and shake him. She really doesn't want to have to drag every word from the man this morning.

'Did he kill Ger?'

The words surprise Anna. But part of her has needed to ask the question. *The* question. She keeps her eyes locked on the sergeant.

'We don't think so, Anna, no.'

For a moment the world goes quiet and the floor drops away beneath Anna. She grips the side of her chair, glad of its solidity, as something intangible collapses within her.

*She's still alive.*

'The lads got him to talk last night. Once he started they couldn't get him to stop. Lonely old cratur, by all accounts. A bit disturbed, you know?'

Anna nods her head and blinks back tears as sweet relief rushes through her veins. The cop takes her silence as his signal to keep talking.

'Not long after his father died, things went downhill with the stepmother — Lorna Cassidy — and she kicked him out. I spoke to the Senior Sergeant down there first thing this morning and he was able to fill me in on a little of the history. Cassidy allegedly threatened her with a knife, pushed her around a bit. A real charmer. She took a protection order against him and he had to move out. But he hung around like a bad smell, didn't stray too far from the property. He'd often sleep in the shack you came across. Then when the old lady passed away, he moved back into the family home. It all kicked off late last year. Turns out he had a thing for Eastern European girls. He'd had a few women out to the property where you stayed after the stepmother died. But then, as things progressed, he'd take them to the shack. By all accounts it started fairly standard, as it were.' Rooney shifts in his seat a little. 'Then his tastes shifted into something a bit more BDSM, with an emphasis on the sadism bit. You know, torture, humiliation type stuff...'

Rooney looks a little hesitant, so Anna offers him a nod of encouragement.

'He'd tie them up. Abuse them a bit. Make them cry. Of course he was filming the whole lot, would upload it, made money on the dark web. But then that wasn't enough, and he started to do a bit of knife play. More threats than anything, but sometimes he'd cut off bits of their hair, or clothes. You know, mementos and stuff.'

'Yeah, I saw his little collection.'

'Right. So, anyway, living where he lived, he quickly got a reputation and none of the girls would risk the abuse. So he recently started looking further afield, for fresh blood, as it were.'

'So that's why…'

'That's why he used his late stepmother's house swap account to find fairly remote cottages, typically on the outskirts of a city where he wasn't known. Your gaff fit the bill nicely. Quiet, but with a ready source of sex workers who could come up from North Dublin. He organised a young Romanian woman to come over on Friday. A Serbian woman on Saturday...'

Anna sits back, queasy, as she thinks of Juliette's phone call. That's what the screams were on the weekend. Some poor girls, far from home, desperate for a few Euros, getting tortured and robbed off their dignity.

'To know he was doing that in my home…'

'We're going through his phone records. We'll be talking to the sex workers to try and build a proper profile. But, as I said, we don't believe he's killed anyone. Maybe just a matter of time. Who knows? But Anna, it's a good thing he's on our radar now.'

Anna's brow furrows. 'But what about Ger? Did you ask him about *Ger*? He had a piece of the top she was wearing that night she vanished. And the white van? I saw her talking to someone in a white—'

Rooney puts the pen back on the table and sits back with a sigh. 'He has an alibi for the evening Ger vanished. We're triple-checking it, but it seems pretty watertight. He was in Galway, for the races. Likes to gamble on the horses. Does the same thing every July, so he's certain of the date.' He glances up at her, sheepishly. 'I'm sorry.'

A tightness has taken hold of Anna's chest. Her hands grip the arms of the chair and she struggles to swallow. Joe Rooney is looking beyond her now, nodding someone in. Ponytail enters silently with two overfull cups of milky tea. A look passes between the two cops. It suddenly hits Anna. The atmosphere is all wrong here today. There should be a buzz in the air, phones ringing, a renewed energy in the air. She glances around.

'What's going on?'

As Ponytail turns to leave she places a hand fleetingly on Anna's shoulder. Anna shrugs it off and leans forward, her fingers flat on the desk.

'Joe? I said what's going on?'

The man leans forward and exhales a deep, exhausted sigh.

'Anna, remember I called you yesterday? I asked you to come in.'

'Of course I remember, I'm here aren't I?' Her words hang defensively in the air for a moment while her mind latches itself back to the edge of the quarry yesterday. She can still see the man she mistook for Dan coming up the ridge towards her in the rain.

*Anna, we need you to come to the station immediately.*

Rooney's words had been lost in the madness of yesterday, but now as they come back to Anna she looks at him. Her vision blurs at the edges. Rooney's hand hovers above his desk, as if he's tempted to move it towards Anna's. He drops it back on the desk.

'Anna,' he pauses, choosing his words carefully, 'yesterday, late morning, a local dog walker was up in the grounds of the abandoned hotel development on the Coast Road...'

Anna realises she is holding her breath.

'… they found something. I'm sorry, Anna, but there was a body in a shallow grave. A woman's body.'

Anna blinks at the grey tea in the paper cup in front of her. She wonders if she can scream herself awake.

'… quite exposed, and with all the recent rain it's not easy for us to identify the victim…'

Anna could stand up, right now, and just walk out of here. Stop his words from reaching her ears. She could run and never stop.

'…wearing a t-shirt, so not a top like the one you described,' he's riffling through his notes, 'an ivory-coloured halter neck top… so there's every chance it's not Ger.'

*It's not Ger. It's not Ger. It's not Ger.*

Anna clings to the words, a lifeline which will stop her going under. She could collapse on the ugly carpet under the sergeant's desk and weep.

'… evidence of blunt trauma to the back of the head. Unfortunately at this stage the face is a little…' He clears his throat. 'The lads in Forensics are waiting on dental records to ID the body. Should be here soon.'

A silence stretches between them. Anna keeps her eyes on the tea. She wishes Dan was here.

'Anna?'

She forces herself to raise her gaze, sees the humanity in his tired eyes. But Anna doesn't want sympathy or kindness. She wants certainty.

'Irrespective of who it is, this is a murder investigation.'

Behind her Ponytail is hovering.

*A murder investigation.*

'But it's not Ger, right? You said—'

'We'll know in the next few hours. But Anna, let's be realistic. There's a chance it could be.'

192

Anna suddenly needs out, claustrophobic in the tight space. She stands abruptly, the chair toppling behind her.

'Anna?'

She grabs her jacket and scarf and pushes her way out through the counter hatch. Rooney is on her heels.

'Anna?'

She's out the blue door and halfway down the path, but his stern words chase her.

'Don't go anywhere. And tell Dan we need to see him. Today.'

# THIRTY-TWO

DAN DIGS HIS KNEE INTO THE SUITCASE and struggles the zip closed with his good hand. A little rivulet of cold sweat runs down his spine as he straightens up. He exhales sharply through his cheeks, but there is no calm to be found. Through narrowed eyes, he takes another furtive glance through his window, then steps back and surveys the sparsely furnished bedroom one last time. Six months he's rented this place, half his nights here, the other half in Anna's. Now it looks exactly as it did the day he arrived, tired and shoddy, no trace of him remaining. He nods to himself, then wheels the suitcase out into the living room. He pulls the bedroom door closed. He hopes the two lads he shares the flat with will just assume he's staying at Anna's for a few nights.

Since listening to Anna's voicemail earlier, a bubble of tension has been expanding in his gut and now it's begun to drum insistently against his chest cavity.

*Rooney wants to see you.*

Dan checks the time on his phone again. He must remain calm. Mistakes happen when people rush. In the past hour he's struggled not to do something stupid. His first instinct was to bring forward his flight from Thursday. But how would that look? He'll leave the flights as they are, and will just have to suck up the wasted cost of the fare. His priority now is to do absolutely nothing to alert them to his intentions.

He stands by his suitcase, a knot of tension pulsing between his shoulder blades, and takes one last look around the squalid little living room with its ugly pleather sofa, the grimy coffee table, the X-box and the wobbly TV stand. He won't miss this place at all. Is it any wonder he ended up spending so many of his evenings up the road in the relative luxury of Anna and Ger's house.

He hasn't had anything to eat yet today, but the thought of food makes him want to hurl. He forces down a few gulps of water from a used mug in the kitchen. Some of it runs down his chin and he discards the rest of it into the sink, watching it swirl and vanish down the plughole, a simple disappearing act. He hopes it's that easy.

One final look out the window. A cluster of lanky schoolkids stuff their faces outside the chipper across the street. A young mother with a nice rack is ploughing past them with a double buggy. Outside the florists, two pensioners are having a natter. Buses chug past in both directions. Nothing unusual. No sign of the cops. He rolls his shoulders back and tells himself that everything is okay. He just needs to hold it together. In a few hours he'll be on the Piccadilly line, heading into the heaving masses of Central London, just another face in the crowd.

In his mind, he quickly runs through his plan once more. He'll max out his card at the ATM down on the street. Then he'll jump on the airport bus and pay in cash for a flight to Heathrow. He can lay low in London for a couple of days, have some breathing space, make a proper plan. Maybe then he'll go some place warm until things blow over. Portugal or Sicily.

His only belonging not yet packed is the yellow Helly Hansen waterproof jacket that Anna got him. He unhooks it from the back of the front door now and slips his bandaged hand into the arm. He zips up the jacket and checks his wallet is in his jeans. He grabs his phone from on top of the suitcase. He'll turn it off in a minute, to stop them tracking him, to minimise his digital footprint. He's not stupid. But before that he has to make one last call. She answers on the first ring.

'Hey, I'm glad you called back. Are you able to make it later? Ger's folks are coming down and I don't think I can see them on my own. I'm really struggling, Dan.'

'It's okay, Banana. Look, I'll try my best. I'm just crazy busy finishing up here at the site.'

'I know. I'm sorry to ask. Just try your best, yeah? The body they found... I don't think it's Ger. I won't believe it's her. This woman... she wasn't wearing a top like Ger had on, you know? So...'

He can hear her swallowing, can tell she's barely holding it together. His mind is blank, he says nothing.

'Dan, I just need you here for when the forensics results come in, can you do that?'

*What's one more white lie.*

'Sure, love. I'll be there.'

There's a pause on the line. He can imagine her lip quivering as she fights off tears. As he stands by his suitcase, he can smell a waft of this morning's sweat off his flannel shirt. But something else, too. And he wonders if it's the reek of shame oozing from his pores. Anna deserves better. She deserves a proper goodbye. And for the most fleeting of moments, he toys with the idea of telling her, explaining what happened, putting her out of her misery. But instead he glances at his watch.

'Did you call the cops? Rooney wants to see you.'

Dan rubs the back of his neck with his bandaged hand. 'No, not yet. Too busy, love. But if you see him, tell him I'll definitely swing by first thing in the morning, yeah?'

'Okay. Good. I'm sure it's just a formality.'

She suddenly sounds distracted, bustling around at something in the background.

'What you doing, love?'

'What? Oh, I'm just loading up my backpack for the beach. I picked up a birthday cake to have with the Kellys. Did I tell you it's Ger's birthday? And a flask of tea. I could do without it, to be honest. Oh, look at these…'

Dan's drumming his fingers on the suitcase. Time to go.

'…I forgot we bought these.'

'What's that, love?' He'll humour her for another moment. This is their last conversation, after all.

'That weekend we went to Berlin. Late May, wasn't it? We bought all those postcards and never got a chance to send them. I might stick them on the fridge. God, I should have cleaned this bag out already…'

She's flustered, eager for distraction. He knows her better than she knows herself.

'Banana, I gotta go. See you later, okay?'

'Okay, love. We'll be at the North Strand. See you shortly. Love you.'

And with that, she's gone. Dan drops the phone to his side and breathes out a long sigh of relief. That's one chapter closed. Another thing ticked off his list. He did love Anna. Or at least he thought he did. But this morning, something seismic has shifted inside him, and now it's like the blinkers have instantly fallen from his eyes. Dan's realised he's been in a bit of a three-month stupor. But that's over now. He could kick himself for hanging around this long, for leaving himself exposed, for risking everything. His survival instinct had told him to play it cool, to not invite suspicion by trying to leave the country without a legit reason. But now, just as his visa's about to expire and he has that legit reason to leave, it's all gone tits up. He snorts at the incredibly bad timing. Why couldn't things have just come to a head in a few days' time.

He turns to the three-quarter length mirror fixed to the inside of the apartment door. As he takes a good hard look at his reflection, he tells himself he can do this, and nods once. One final glance over his shoulder into the crummy flat, then he wheels the suitcase out and pulls the door firmly closed.

Outside on the street, it's as if every pair of eyes is trained on him. He trundles his case the short distance to the ATM and taps in his PIN. The maximum he can withdraw is a couple of thousand Euros, enough to last him a week or so, if he's clever with it. He zips the cash into the inside pocket of his jacket, then pulls the suitcase in the direction of the bus stop in front of the post office. The rolling sound of the case on the pavement makes people turn and stare. Or maybe he's just being paranoid. He attempts an air of indifference as he reaches the bus stop and glances down the street. No sign of the airport bus. Should he wait in the post office? But that might draw even more attention. He glances up and down the drab street. Over on the far side of the road, one of the pensioners seems to be staring across at him. Dan looks away, pretends to read something on his phone. He holds in the power button until the phone shuts down. Another look up the street. Where is this bloody bus?

As he picks distractedly at the bandage on his hand, he runs through everything in his head once more, unable to shake a niggling feeling that he's forgotten something. His mouth is dry but he won't risk buying a bottle of water in case the bus comes. For some reason he's thinking back to the conversation with Anna. At least he's leaving her with some happy memories. That trip to Berlin feels like a different lifetime ago. And it makes him happy to know that soon he'll be off on new foreign adventures again. He's had enough of this place, way too much baggage. Another quick glance up the street and a giddy relief runs through him as the airport bus swings around the corner into view. He can do this. Just thirty minutes and he'll be at the airport ticket desk.

As the bus chugs closer, Dan allows his shoulders to relax. He thinks of Anna, hopes in time she can forgive him. She wasn't a bad sort. He grabs the handle of his suitcase, forcing his knuckles to relax their tight grip, then sidles closer to the kerbside. He'll sit up the back, less chance of being noticed. The bus chugs closer.

*Wallet.*

*Phone.*

*Cash.*

*Passp—*

The blood drains from his face.

*His fucking passport.*

His chest thumps as the bus pulls in with a pneumatic hiss. The doors fling open, disgorging people from the back. Others grumble as they drag their own suitcases around the man in the yellow jacket who's blocking their way. But Dan can't move. He stands in a daze. And now he knows why he was thinking of Berlin. He can still see it, where he asked her to store it, in the little inside zipped pocket, while they waited for their bags at the luggage carousel. His passport is still in her fucking backpack.

The bus driver looks at him, a tired eyebrow raised.

Dan says nothing. Just a tight shake of his head.

The bus pulls off. Dan swallows as he realises what he's now going to have to do.

*Fuck!*

# THIRTY-THREE

ANNA'S BEEN IN THE SEA TOO LONG. Her limbs are slow, her toes and fingers numb from the cold. She's treading water, the furthest out she's ever ventured, hoping it's far enough from the stony shoreline of the North Strand for the Kellys not to see the worry etched on her face. Her breathing is laboured and the saltwater has begun to sting the grazed skin of her throat. Ger's parents sit waiting on a bench, Anna's backpack beside them. Even from here, through salt-stung eyes, Anna can see the wretched expressions on their faces. They haven't taken out the flask of hot tea yet, probably waiting on Anna to come back in. The birthday cake was a stupid idea. It's still boxed up in the bottom of the backpack and none of them will be in the mood to eat it. Just last week, when Anna had invited the Kellys down to mark Ger's birthday, it had been a spontaneous idea during a phone call. A nice, well-meant gesture at the time. But now, Anna feels ill with tension, unable to not think of the woman's body awaiting identification on a slab in the police morgue, dental records about to tell them if it's Ger or not. For all she knows the forensics might have already been completed, the results at this minute speeding through the ether to Rooney's inbox. Anna's stomach tightens under the cold water. She must stay positive, it will all be over soon. At least Dan is coming. He'll be a welcome distraction, will keep the conversation trickling, anything to stop them all from obsessing.

Anna turns her body. Ten or so meters away, a lone seagull crawks as it lands on top of the outboard motor of an anchored dive boat. A few minutes ago, Anna had watched as the instructor and two of his pupils flopped backwards off the side of the boat, cocooned in neoprene dry suits, their faces obscured by scuba masks and exposure hoods. She glances down but can see no sign of them below, the visibility of the water next to nothing today. The gull takes flight from the end of the boat. As Anna watches it head off towards the old stone pier and the docked trawlers, her teeth begin an insistent chatter. She should have worn her own neoprene today. Another minute. Just one more minute to steel herself for what lies ahead.

As she fans her hands back and forth through the water, Rooney's earlier words barge into her mind.

*A body in a shallow grave.... evidence of blunt trauma to the back of the head...*

Anna twists away from the words, looks across to the Mourne Mountains in the distance, their outline barely visible through thin cloud. Since that night in July, she's had a constant inner dialogue with herself, has instantly snuffed out any notions that Ger might be dead. An exercise in denial, her mind has clung to any multitude of reasons for Ger's disappearance. But now she feels an overwhelming nausea at the realisation her defences might be about to be torn down.

Her mouth dips below the water's surface. Sensation is rapidly deserting her limbs. It's time to head back in. She kicks harder with both legs and swooshes her arms so she turns to face the strand and Ger's parents once more. She's on the point of pulling herself into a front crawl when she hesitates, something snagging on her subconscious. A colour. She looks off slightly to the right of the bench, her focus trailing along the promenade, and feels a rush of relief as she recognises a shock of bright yellow moving along at a fast clip. Dan is here, his raincoat momentarily flaring like a beacon as he quickly walks through a fleeting shaft of sunlight, carrying himself with a no-nonsense energy. But something isn't right. He's now at the bench and his hand has gone straight to Anna's backpack. Ger's parents have turned to look at him, but Dan appears to ignore them, his face pale, an urgency to his actions. Anna considers shouting his name, asking him what's wrong, but she already knows her broken voice won't carry that far. So instead she watches, confused, and with an escalating sense of unease, as a deep frown furrows her brow. Dan has flipped the backpack and now shakes it roughly, the flask sliding out and clipping the edge of the bench on its way down to the slab of concrete underneath. And now the boxed-up cake tumbles out, exploding at Assumpta's feet. The Kellys move away from the bench a little, stunned at what's unfolding in front of them. And just then Dan seems to find what's he's been searching for. He slips something into his jacket pocket, then glances out towards Anna, his eyes on hers for no longer than a split second. But even that quick look is enough to chill Anna in a way the seawater hasn't managed. He sets the empty backpack on the bench, then turns to retrace his steps back along the promenade, breaking into a slow jog, when he comes to an abrupt stop.

Two uniformed cops are approaching from the near distance on the right. Behind them, struggling to keep up, is Ponytail. Dan turns on his heel and his face pales further. Anna follows his gaze and sees what he's just seen: Rooney and two additional uniformed Guards approaching steadily from the opposite end of the prom. Rooney is barking something into a radio as they advance. The Kellys have their backs to Anna, but they cling to each other now. Even from here, Anna can see the wild panic in Dan's eyes. He's a trapped beast, desperate for an escape route. He turns then, looks beyond her, his eyes sweeping the horizon. And then something settles in his expression.

Dan pelts down to the water's edge, his raincoat cast behind him, his shoes kicked off in seconds. His eyes are locked on Anna, a grim determination on his face, as he bounds into the chill water still clad in his jeans and shirt. Anna will swim to him, meet him halfway, find out what the hell is going on. He'll explain everything, make it all okay. But she cannot move. A survival mechanism in her reptilian brain has taken over, has frozen her limbs so that they hang motionless, anchoring her to the spot.

In the background Assumpta watches on, a hand raised to her heart. Further up the prom, near the boat ramp, one of the young male cops is trying to commandeer a jetski from the back of a locked trailer. Rooney is dragging a kayak down from someone's back garden, its base scraping and bumping over the stony surface of the strand. Another of the cops is at the shoreline now, cursing as he fumbles at his shoelaces, his eyes tracking Dan.

'Pell! Stop!'

But Dan has no intention of stopping. Anna watches as he cuts through the water, his bandaged hand and clothes barely slowing him down. She loses track of time, the light around her dulling, a nightmare eeriness infiltrating the air around her. She is paralysed, useless, helpless. Dan comes to a stop, mere metres from her. He glances back to check the cops' progress.

'I'm sorry, Banana.' He's panting, the sleeves of his flannel shirt blurry drags beneath the water's surface.

'What are you talking about?'

He's distracted, looking beyond her, his jaw set, something impenetrable in his expression.

'Dan?' Anna's voice is raspy and unsure, the word barely a whisper, suspended between them over the low chop of the water. She repeats it, hears the hidden plea her tone imparts in its single syllable.

He looks directly at her now, holds her gaze, as if incredulous the penny hasn't yet dropped.

'Dan, what did you do?' Anna tastes bile in the back of her throat. The man in front of her is at once familiar and unknown. She glances back towards the shore, fighting a rising sense of panic. At the shoreline Rooney is pushing the younger cop out of his way, insisting on clambering into the kayak himself. But he's nowhere near her. None of them are. And in that moment Anna has never felt more afraid in her life.

Dan sweeps his arms and edges his body towards her, closing the distance. 'It wasn't my fault.'

# July

# THIRTY-FOUR

DAN SPARKED UP A JOINT by the sliding back door and leaned against the cool outside wall. He'd just dropped Anna like a sack of spuds on the bed and now he smirked to himself as he thought of her passed out face down, singsong mumbling giving way to heavy snoring. She was cute when pissed and he was quietly impressed by the amount of booze his woman could put away. She must have sank a gallon of wine in Mulligan's this evening and she'd feel rough as guts tomorrow. At least she'd been smart enough to book the day off work.

He glanced over towards the kitchen clock. It had just gone midnight and he'd be up in less than six hours for a day on the building site. But at least it was Friday, and he'd be long gone by the time Anna woke up with her monster hangover. He exhaled a long steady stream of heady smoke up towards the clear sky and felt his shoulders soften against the wall. The moon was a few days away from full, but with the house in darkness, Dan observed the blanket of stars overhead. They were good, but they weren't a patch on the stars back home.

In the distance, through the hedge, he could just make out a light come on in Juliette's kitchen window. He'd often wondered what the old neighbour would be like between the sheets. A single mother in her mid-forties, she'd probably be well up for it. What was it one of the lads on the site had said recently? A woman in her forties who'd squeezed out a brood of kids would probably have a badly packed kebab down below. On hearing that, Dan had snorted chocolate milk out his nose, and now found himself chuckling quietly again.

Above him, a floorboard creaked. The sound wasn't coming from Anna's room. Dan groaned.

*Oh great.*

Earlier that evening, Ger had had a face on her like a smashed crab when she'd spotted Dan and Gav stumbling into the pub. The frostiness had been unmistakable. Now, standing on the patio, Dan tapped the back of his left boot against the wall and wondered just what was her problem with her boss. It wasn't just this evening either. She'd been frosty for a while now. Dan took another slow drag, watched the tip of the joint flare and dim, and thought back to this evening and how she'd bolted from the pub like her arse was on fire. He picked a loose strand of tobacco from his lip and flicked it into the near gloom of the garden. Poor Gavin. He was harmless really. Ger just needed to give him a break.

The middle stair creaked. Dan took another toke and waited quietly in the stillness.

'Oh. You're up.'

There it was: the frostiness again.

'I am.'

She was at the fridge, the door open, her body bathed in yellow light as she filled her glass from the filter jug. She was dressed for bed, wearing her loose baggy grey t-shirt and a pair of skimpy shorts. Dan's eyes lingered appreciatively on her long, tanned legs. Even without a scrap of make-up, Ger was drop dead gorgeous. She always had been. Just a damn shame she had such a stick up her arse.

She closed the fridge and turned to leave.

*Fuck it.*

'Ger, wait up. Is there a problem?'

She stopped, her back to him, her shoulders braced. Dan flicked the end of the joint into the back garden and stepped into the kitchen.

'What do you mean?' she said coolly.

*So it's like that.*

She kept her back to him. He paused for a moment, the edges of his brain a little fuzzy from the joint. He hated this shit. Why couldn't women just be direct?

'I dunno. You seemed a bit off when Gav and me arrived at the pub earlier. You seem a bit off now too, if I'm honest. Has Gav done something else to piss you off? I can have a word with him, if you like.'

Dan's hand moved up the wall by the sliding door and found the switch for the outdoor light. The sudden harshness of the glare bouncing off the flagstones outside made him squint for a moment. He took a step towards her, the light contaminating the space between them, and saw her hands balled into tight fists.

'Ha!'

A single syllable. Bitchy, annoying. A ripple of tension passed across Dan's jaw. Something was about to go down and he wasn't firing on all cylinders after the booze and the smoke. But fuck it. He was more that able to handle whatever her problem was. She turned now, a steely stare, her own jaw set in defiance. They held each other's gaze, a game of chicken, until he blinked and looked away. For some reason his eyes ended up on her tits and she sighed a long patronising sigh as she folded her arms to cover herself. She took a step towards him.

'Is there a problem, he says ...'

Dan locked his eyes on her again, his own arms folded. He'd say nothing. Make her uncomfortable with the silence. She'd raised an eyebrow in invitation.

'No? Okay then, I'll tell you what the problem is, if you're really that clueless, Dan.'

She was standing so close he could feel the warmth of her breath. There was something surreal about the moment and he was properly stoned now. Perhaps she was about to tell him she fancied him. That would explain everything. He picked up his half-drunk beer bottle from the table and took a long slug. This could be interesting.

'I saw you.'

'What?'

'I saw you. Two weeks ago.'

'Okay …' Dan had seriously not one clue what this mad bint was talking about. But he'd let her ramble away if it chilled her out a bit.

She shifted the weight onto her other hip. 'Two weeks ago, I was in town seeing a client. Nothing unusual there. But as I was rushing up Fade Street, who do I spot just inside Hogan's but a very cosy looking couple …'

*Fuck.*

'An older woman, blonde, very… how should I put this… *handsy*. I didn't think older blondes were your type, Dan. But then, what do I know?'

The kitchen was suddenly airless and hot. Dan stood rigid, trying to look impassive, sweat prickling his scalp. He'd deny it, tell her she'd got it wrong.

'But I guess the real question, Danny-boy, is, what does *Anna* know?'

He needed a moment. He picked up his bottle for another swig but it was empty. He put it down clumsily and it toppled to the floor.

'It was a one-off. It won't—'

'Ha!'

That fucking noise again.

'There's no way in hell that was a one-off, Dan. You were all over each other like a rash, in broad daylight. You're a fucking pig, and it's taken every ounce of strength for me not to tell Anna.' There were tears brimming in her eyes now, and she was shaking with rage. Fuck, he hated drama.

His finger jutted out and poked her sharply in the shoulder blade.

'You leave Anna out of this!'

She was looking down at his finger, still pressed into her shoulder, an expression of utter disbelief on her face. And then her eyes were back on him, blazing. She launched at him, pushing him back with both hands.

'How fucking dare you touch me!'

'Would you shut up, for God's sake,' he shout-whispered at her urgently. 'You'll wake Anna.'

'Ha! Would that be so bad? She has a right to know. She trusts you and you act like an utter gobshite. Actually that's an insult to gobshites. You're a loser, Dan. An absolute loser!'

She had him backed against the wall, her spittle flying in his face as she raged on.

'You're going to have to tell her. I won't let you lie to her anymore, Dan. I'm done with your bullshit.'

Her finger was pointed in his face now. Dan's foot clipped the empty beer bottle and sent it skidding across the slate tiles. His chest tightened as he struggled for air. He needed space. He stepped forward and pushed her firmly back.

'I said don't touch me!'

Ger's open palm whacked his cheek. It took his foggy brain a moment to register that she'd slapped him. She stepped back, her breathing heavy, and wiped the back of her hand along her mouth. But she hadn't finished with him. Cogs whirred behind her eyes, and now she was turning to glance over her shoulder. The door into the front hall was ajar. And Dan knew what's coming. She turned back to face him.

'You're going to tell her, Dan. Right now. Anna!'

What happened next was pure reflex, his boxing training taking over. His fist darted out, connected with Ger's chin. She stumbled backwards.

*Shit.*

He pulled his hand back as if it had been scalded. A stunned silence hung between them. Ger raised a hand to her face, momentarily shell-shocked. Dan's groggy thoughts stumbled to their feet. He'd apologise. Calm her down and defuse the situation before she woke up Anna. But she was looking at him now, a storm flaring behind her eyes, as she sucked in air, swelling in rage, an explosion imminent.

'I'm sorry Ger—'

She looked him right in the eye and emptied her lungs.

'Anna!'

It happened in a blur. Dan's uppercut struck her jaw with full force. Ger's feet lifted off the floor and time seemed to stretch as her body traced a slow arc towards the slate floor of the kitchen. Dan held his breath as he watched but looked away at the last moment. A sickening thud filled the silent kitchen and he knew it was Ger's skull hitting the tiles. He forced himself to crack open his eyes and stood dazed, observing, his clenched fist slowly unfurling by his side. Adrenaline rushed through his body and he staggered out of his stupor. And then he, too, was on the floor, gently pulling Ger upwards by the shoulders. Her head hung limp and a glossy patch of darkness had started a slow expansion across the slate floor where her head had made contact.

'No, no, no.'

He lay her carefully down again and leaned in to listen. She was breathing, just. He picked her up like a dozing baby and carefully manoeuvred her through the doorway and up the hall. Now it was Dan's turn to shout.

'Anna? Anna!'

He propped Ger on the bottom stairs and ran up to Anna's room. Anna was exactly as he left her, snoring and comatose, face in pillow, arse in air. She was of no use. He bolted back down the stairs, his heart pounding, and crouched down beside Ger. Her face was paling by the minute.

*Think, Dan. Think.*

Anna would only slow him down. As he stood by the front door, tears started to run down his cheeks, but he had no free hand to wipe them away. The hospital in Drogheda was half an hour away. If he floored it they might make it in twenty. He carefully put Ger's feet onto the hallway floorboards and patted the front pocket of his jeans to check his car keys were there. He pulled open the front door. Ger's legs offered no support and he had to carefully swing her lower body outside. He pulled the front door closed behind them, then bent to scoop up Ger's legs, jostling her into a snug hold in his arms. The scent of her shampoo filled his nose, but something else too, something metallic. As he raced them to the car, a patch of warmth spreads across his shoulder where her head was lolling. The faintest breath and whimper escaped her lips and struggled weakly into the still night air.

# THIRTY-FIVE

THE STREETS LAY DESERTED. Dan drove in stops and starts, flying along the road, then braking at the last minute for speed bumps. He wound down the window to shake off any lingering grogginess from the beer and spliff. A brisk wind blew in from the shoreline. He glanced over to the passenger seat as the car cornered onto the Balbriggan Road. Ger's body was starting to slump towards him and he reached out to bolster her back up.

He borrowed his hand back to gear down for another speed bump, cursing himself for not reclining the passenger seat before they set off. He shifted up to fourth, then started to accelerate them away from the village, past sleeping houses with curtains drawn. To his right, shards of moonlight danced on the water. He risked another look to his left and a chill ran through him. Ger was looking at him, but her open eyes had a glassiness to them and seemed to simply stare into the middle distance, as if she had deserted her body.

'Ger? Ger, mate. Just hold on, we're nearly there, okay?'

But they were still miles from the hospital. A strange noise — part groaning, part pleading — rose up from somewhere and it took Dan a moment to realise it was coming from him.

Up ahead, on the right, he spotted the car park, a bare patch of gravel just off the roadside, nothing beyond it but some scraggly bushes tumbling down to the sea. He'd been here once or twice to drop off their recycling in the bins near the entrance. Right now, it was deserted. Pulling in, he killed the engine, then rushed around to the passenger side. He opened the car door, fast but careful, and gently turned Ger's face towards him.

His eyes scanned the outline of her face. Her lips were slightly parted and her hair was tied back in its usual loose ponytail. But her skin was a sickly ashen-white and her face stayed tilted at an uncomfortable angle when he took his hand away. Dan stepped back, his legs weak. A wave of nausea roiled through his gut.

*This can't be happening.*

He leaned back in, his fingers trembling as they pressed into the cool soft skin of her neck, a desperate hunt for a hint of a pulse. But no sign of life appeared under his fingertips. He grabbed an old plastic water bottle discarded at Ger's feet and tipped some water over his hands, then patted his damp palms repeatedly against her cheeks. No response. He gripped her jaw and gave her a bit of a shake.

'Come on, Ger. Stay with me…'

He watched, his breath held, begging for a sign. In the background, invisible waves continued their distant grumble and swoosh, but inside, Dan's brain had begun to roar. Could he still bomb it down the road to the hospital? Was there a chance they might still save her? He dropped his gaze to the shadows, the patch of Ger's blood on his shoulder now cold against his skin.

In a movie, this is the part when Ger would gasp herself awake, suddenly alert, her wide eyes searching for his. And Dan would collapse in a mess of relief, a thousand thank yous to the Gods above. He squeezed his eyes shut and shook his head. This wasn't a movie. Seconds passed and the waves in the background continued their suck and kiss. He forced his eyes open. There was no running from this cold reality. She was gone. He slumped forward, his knees on the gravel.

*Think, Dan.*

He could call the cops, explain what happened. Surely they'd understand? If he phoned them now, got them down here, while her body was still warm... Time was of the essence, and any delay would look dodgy. But even as his hands drifted to his pocket, he could already see his phone still charging back in Anna's room beside her bed. He cursed himself, stood and paced away from the car, then back again.

He crouched down once more, close to her body. It had been many years since he'd mumbled a prayer, but he cobbled one together now. As he took Ger's limp hand in search of forgiveness, a heaving sob took over his body and he struggled to gulp it back down. His shoulders shuddered. But he forced onwards with his words, until he could no longer ignore the panic rising inside. His frantic words tumbled over each other, evolving in need, their target morphing, so that soon he was no longer seeking Ger's forgiveness, but instead was begging God for another chance.

He stepped back from the body and wiped the useless tears of frustration from his eyes. What was going to happen to him now? He slapped his hand against his forehead. And again, harder still. He'd killed Ger and there wasn't a judge in the country who wouldn't lock him up for years. He was only twenty eight years old, for God's sake. He wasn't ready for his life to be over. It was just a stupid accident.

The fresh air and adrenaline had fully sobered him up by now. He stood up tall and looked to the night sky, to those very same stars he'd admired from the patio door only thirty minutes ago. A different lifetime ago. He rubbed the heel of both hands into his eye sockets. His world had just tipped off its axis and all he wanted was to shove it back into its rightful position. His fingers intertwined and formed a steeple behind his neck. Surely this couldn't be how his life came to an end.

A distant hum grew louder and a moment later a pair of headlights swept over the car. Dan crouched lower as the vehicle continued on its way. He remained there, his thoughts melding with the to and fro of the waves in the background. And he waited for something to guide him, to fix this, to undo what would be the biggest regret of his life. But only one quiet conclusion bubbled insistently to the surface. And it was that there was simply no point in two lives ending tonight.

He stood and looked down at the lifeless body slumped in the passenger seat. His jaw tensed. Why did she have to be so mouthy? Why couldn't she just have minded her own bloody business? He shook his head at the utter needlessness of what had happened. He knew he should have just walked away when Ger arced up back in the kitchen. He shouldn't have hit her. That was wrong. He knew that, yet... He looked down at her face, the mouth hanging open, the glazed eyes looking through him, still holding a hint of reproach. He scuffed his shoe against the tarmac. Daft woman. He took no pleasure in saying it, but she brought this on herself. He stepped back from the car. There was no way he was going to let this destroy his life too. And in that moment, he knew what he had to do. What choice did he have?

He cocked an ear, but no cars were coming. The flinty light of the waxing moon drew his eye over to the construction site across the road. He'd passed this place countless times, a plot cleared of rocks, foundations not yet built, now mucky and weed strewn. The grounds for the proposed hotel, whose plans had been scuppered, stopped in its tracks by petitions wielded by people like Ger. A weather-faded sign, a couple of years old, still heralded the forthcoming hotel that would never come forth. Dan rubbed a hand down his tired face, popped open the boot and surveyed the clutter of tools he used for work. He selected a pair of gloves and grabbed a shovel. His jaw was set in silent determination now, and with the familiarity of the shovel in his grip a calm resolve settled over him. He leaned into the car and hoisted Ger's body up efficiently over his shoulder, then carried her steadily across the road. The bottom of her tee-shirt fluttered across the top of her thighs. He clambered carefully up the ditch and over the broken earth and stony ruts towards the far corner of the abandoned building site. Nature had already started to reclaim her patch of earth with spindly weeds and tufts of rye grass. A squat blackthorn tree hunkered low by an old stone wall at a point furthest from the road. That's where he'd put her. He laid the corpse down on the ground and started to dig, a steadfast focus as the blade of the spade rasped at the soil. When he put her in the hole, he'd be sure to turn her face so the dirt didn't go in her eyes. After all, he told himself, he wasn't a monster.

# October

# THIRTY-SIX

'IT WASN'T MY FAULT.'

Dan's treading water, within reach now, their ragged breaths filling the air between them. Anna's shoulders have begun to shake as warm tears streak her cheeks. A cold ache burns her lungs. Her energy reserves are depleted. He edges closer through the water and Anna's heart wants to implode.

'It was an accident.'

Anna's head shakes involuntarily, as if she can somehow block out his words. Not this. Please God, not this.

'I tried to get her to the hospital…but she…'

Anna presses her lips together, scrunches her eyes shut to close out this reality. An animal cry rushes up from her core and takes flight into the clouded blue above. Something crumbles and fragments inside her and her body tumbles through space. She yearns for sudden oblivion. In this moment, all Anna can imagine is her friend's beautiful face, rotted and weathered now, her toe tagged, a lifeless body on a cold metal table. She coughs out a ragged sob, then chokes as her lungs judder and gasp for air. As she flails up, spluttering, the cruellest movie reel flickers to life in her mind: that sunny day at the market back in April. The handsome stranger with an open shirt and a cheeky smile. The cafe she brought him to. Ger waiting with her crossword. Image after image of the day they met comes flooding back, each a stinging slice across Anna's soul. Because it was Anna who brought him into their lives. She wants to die but she needs to hear it.

'What did you do?' Her words are almost inaudible, but they hit their target.

'Anna...'

He looks pathetic. She needs to turn away. Her eyes find the Mourne Mountains once more.

'Tell me what you did.' Her voice is louder and steady now, to hell with her ruined throat.

'I came to tell you. That's why I'm here.'

Anna says nothing, her gaze fixed on the mountains. She thinks of his mad rummage in the backpack a few minutes ago. And she remembers now what item was still stored away in the inside pocket. He isn't here to confess anything. He's only here for his passport so he can disappear. She turns her body and stares at him. 'What did you do to Ger?'

He's looking down at his bandaged hand as it swooshes back and forth in the water. The sleeves of his flannel shirt cling to his forearms, his jeans blur. There's a tortured anguish on his face, but Anna can already see it begin to fade, a cold, clinical expression shoving it out of the way.

'We argued.'

'You argued.'

He's picking at the submerged bandage. 'She was going to wake you.'

In the background, Rooney is advancing awkwardly on the kayak. He'll be a while yet. In front of her, Dan has a resentful look on his face, like each word said is a favour. His voice is low, a mumble to the surface of the water. 'She saw me with someone else.'

He looks at Anna now, puppy dog eyes, his limbs coaxing his body slowly forwards. Anna tries to make a fist, but all sensation has left her hands. The chatter in her teeth is almost comical.

'What happened?' Anna watches him, needing to know, but sick at the thought of knowing.

A familiar voice echoes over the water. Ponytail has sourced a loudspeaker somewhere. Her amplified words bounce over the water, but neither of them listens. Anna keeps her eyes on the bastard in front of her.

'I pushed her.' His eyes drill imploringly into her. 'It was an accident, Anna. I swear it.' He looks away, his brow etched in a crisscross of discomfort. 'She fell.' He doesn't want to be here, to do this. 'She was going crazy. I had to defend myself.'

His bandaged hand moves through the water, softly breaks the surface and lands tentatively on Anna's shoulder. Her insides tighten and every cell in her body seems to shrink in on itself. He's using his good hand to manoeuvre himself a few inches closer.

'Get away from her, Pell!' Rooney is ploughing up the water with his paddle, still twenty or so meters away. Dan throws a quick glance over his shoulder at the approaching cop, surveys the progress of the other cops at their various positions on the shoreline. Rooney is the only one who's nearby, the most pressing threat. Dan glances beyond Anna to the anchored dive boat again, his expression calculating. That's why he swam out here. Any moment now the prick is going to make a run for it, start up the motor and disappear. She doesn't have long.

'It was an accident?' She tries to keep her tone neutral.

'Yes. It was stupid, really. She brought it on herself.'

His good hand comes towards Anna's face. As his fingers gently sweep some strands of wet hair away from her forehead, Anna has an overwhelming urge to vomit. She invited this monster into her home, she let him into her bed, she had him inside her body. And without her, Ger would still be here.

He briefly cranes his neck to check on Rooney's progress, readying to depart. 'I just wanted to tell you. To take responsibility, you know?'

Anna nods, let's her cheek rest softly against his bandaged hand. He nods in return, his brow smoothing, forgiveness achieved. It's time for him to go. Anna glides her mouth around to the outside of his hand and clamps down. His yell pierces the sky. But she digs her teeth in harder and tastes the glorious metallic tang of blood as it coats her gums. He tugs violently, but Anna will not leg go. She grinds her jaw.

'Get off me, you mad bitch!'

His other hand meets her cheek, an open palm, then again, a closed fist, hammering down on yesterday's bruises. But Anna is beyond pain. In the background, Rooney is yelling. The water takes on a pink hue in front of Anna's face. The texture in her mouth is no longer just bandage. She's through to flesh. His fist meets her skull again and Anna goes under, the water thrashing, but she's locked on. She'll keep him here until Rooney arrives. Her vision swims as he holds her down. She bites even harder, her last remaining energy focused solely on trapping this hand that killed her friend. She'll cling on forever if she has to, a scourge to hound him through his days, a warning siren to other women. She'll not let Ger down, not again. Suddenly, Dan's knee connects with her chest and she's winded. Her lungs begin to fill as she's jolted backwards underwater. And Dan is free. Anna's face barely breaks the surface. She coughs and chokes.

Rooney is close now, breathing heavily, his face blanched at what he's seeing. The cop's eyes meet Anna's for a split-second. Dan is already at the boat, dragging his body up the dinghy's side with his one good hand, then clambering both upper arms over. He struggles his torso over the side of the boat, then pulls his legs up and over. Anna coughs and gulps, then dips under the surface again. The dinghy's outboard motor turns and splutters into life, the sound dulled by the water in Anna's ears. As she looks up she can see the blur of Rooney's silhouette against the sky, halfway between herself and Dan. And it comforts her to know there are still good men like Rooney out there. She imagines his panicked gaze darting back and forth between herself, drowning, and Dan, escaping, his brain fighting to select the best course of action, each millisecond precious. He must choose. The anchor chain rumbles as Dan releases it into the depths.

For the last time, Anna's face breaks the water's surface for the briefest moment, but her vision has closed in now. Her mouth opens a sliver and she takes in her last sip of air. Then she's under again, no fight left. They say drowning is a peaceful way to go. Slowly, her body sinks backwards into the cold, dark depths. They got the bastard, that's all that matters. The sea can take her now.

# THIRTY-SEVEN

A HUSHED ENERGY ROLLS ALONG HARBOUR ROAD. Lunches are discarded, front doors left ajar, conversations paused. Neighbours lean into murmurs and quiet exclamations.

*Sweet Jesus.*

*Who?*

*Holy mother of God.*

Shoes and trainers, slippers and boots, slowly gather on the pavement around her. Their owners keep a respectful distance, but all feet point like iron filings to a magnet, sympathetic eyes trained on the bedraggled woman bent forward on a stranger's dining chair. Anna keeps her face down. The chair had been hurriedly brought out from a house behind her and its owner has since fetched multiple jackets from the coat stand in her front hall. The latest of these, the elderly Samaritan's husband's navy pea-coat, now forms the top-most layer, an outer skin to quell the chill wracking Anna's body. The wool collar is soft against her neck.

When she closes her eyes, her mind jumps back ten minutes so she can still see the candy-striped beach towel they'd rolled her onto, feel the stones and pebbles through the thin material, her cheek pressed against the damp cotton. Her lungs had purged themselves of never-ending saltwater, the pain in her throat a glassy scald. The diver who'd dragged her in from the sea had squatted in front of her on the shore, and as they'd coaxed Anna back to life, coughing and spluttering on that beach towel, her bloodshot eyes had come to focus on the black rubber crotch of her rescuer's dry suit. An image of the sexless Ken doll she had owned when she was six years old had come to mind. She'd stared at the man's rubber mound, not caring, as they'd gathered and fretted and encouraged more water from her lungs. Funny where the mind goes.

'Will I give her black tea?'

Anna opens her eyes, but she hasn't yet the energy to lift her head. She just needs another minute. She recognises the pair of slippers. Tartan, with a charcoal trim. It's the lady who owns the house behind her, the bringer of chair, the borrower of spouse coats.

'Give her nothing. Her lungs might still have water in them. Wait til the ambulance arrives. Where is the damn thing?'

A pair of leather brogues comes into view, then swiftly moves away again. The slippers move to Anna's side and a hand rests gently on her shoulder.

'It's alright, pet. Not long now.'

Anna's thoughts are still foggy. There were a blissful few seconds, lying in recovery position on the towel, when it hadn't yet come back to her. But then the terrible new reality had slammed into her, her stomach convulsing once more, but for a different reason this time. She listens now, aware of some activity taking place further up the road. Her shoulders rise and fall under the mountain of coats, her weary lungs unsteady, her breath jagged. And she thinks of Ger's parents. The Kellys must be close by. She swallows down the pain in her throat and slowly forces up her head.

It takes her a moment to see through the gathering crowd. But there she is, Ger's mother, standing alone on the other side of the onlookers. She has turned herself away, appears lost in a moment of private torment, her fingers raised to the stippled front wall of a stranger's house, as if that alone will keep her tethered to something solid in this world. As Anna watches, it's as if she can see the dawning weight of the worst type of loss begin to rupture every cell in Assumpta's body. Anna's own heart splinters. She should go to her, comfort her. But she has no energy to shake off the weight of the coats, doesn't trust her legs not to buckle beneath her. Instead she looks away.

*Fished him out.*

*Bastard.*

*Whist. Here they come.*

The feet jostle and turn. Anna's gaze follows. They all stare along Harbour Road in the direction of the pier. There's movement up there. Anna can make out a police car in the distance.

A gangly teen on a bike comes flying down the road, his eyes alight. He skids the bike to a halt only metres from the spot where Anna has been stationed. The boy spots his target in the crowd.

'Da, they pulled him in. He's soaked. And his hands a bloody mess. He's handcuffed in the back of the car. They're—'

'Jonah, would you shush!'

The kid looks momentarily stung, but there's no real rebuke to the father's words. Everyone knows the boy has been silenced out of respect for the woman sitting in their midst. A hush descends as the crowd's focus returns to the cop car. They'll be coming in this direction, then turning left on Strand Street, the Garda station just a stone's throw from here. The car approaches, one of the young male cops solemn behind the wheel. Beside him, Rooney sits wet and dishevelled in the passenger seat, a dazed expression fixed straight ahead. There is not a sound among the crowd.

It's as the cop car nears the turn-off for Strand Street that Ger's father steps forward. The vehicle brakes suddenly. Mister Kelly, now blocking it, places both hands wide on the bonnet and leans forward. His tired eyes stare straight beyond the cops to his daughter's killer in the back seat. He holds his position for a moment, then swiftly rounds the side of the car and pounds on the back window with the flat of his hand, then the side of his fist. His face is puce with fury. His spittle flecks the glass as he curses and shouts at the killer mere inches away. But Daniel, in the back, coolly ignores him, his eyes fixed obstinately on the middle distance, as if the whole fuss is intended for someone else.

'Why?', Mister Kelly roars.

'Why?', he repeats, his words echoing pitifully off the car window, the onlookers silent, dropping their gaze.

Only as the car moves slowly off does the fight seem to leave the man. His big shoulders heave and his face twists in agony. Anna watches from her chair, tears spilling silently down her face, as Phelim Kelly, a rock of a man from her childhood, bends over and wails in the middle of the street, a man forever broken.

Something would die within them all that day, a natural trust in the goodness of the world snuffed out.

That night, Anna awoke in an unfamiliar room. She had no recollection of any discussion with her neighbour, but, nevertheless, here she was in Juliette's spare room. At three o'clock that morning, when Anna stood in the stillness and peered through the bedroom window, she could see the outline of her old home, the roof chalky in the clear light of the crescent moon. With a slight start, she suddenly remembered the poor cats, home alone, no doubt starving. But when she turned to grab her coat, a snatched memory of an earlier conversation came back to her: the Kellys had already taken the cats away with them that evening, back to Drogheda for a new life. Anna hadn't got to say goodbye to either cats or Kellys and as she turned for the window once more she couldn't honestly tell which was more upsetting in that moment. Her thoughts were muddied. She was exhausted but wired. When she took another look across to her old home, she already knew in her bones that she'd never spend another night there. No coat of fresh paint or newly purchased furniture would ever be able to distract from what had gone on within those four walls.

The media interest in the ensuing days had bordered on ferocious. It had startled Anna the next morning, when she'd ventured out to the supermarket, to see Dan's face splashed across the front pages of the national newspapers. She'd made it onto the cover of one tabloid herself. A bolshie journalist had even trailed her from the shops, then door stopped her at Juliette's, angling for a seedy exclusive, a love triangle gone wrong type of thing. Juliette, bless her, had pulled Anna back inside and set the dogs on the prick. But soon enough, as days passed, interest waned. As Mrs Kelly had said to Anna one afternoon, about two weeks after they'd found Ger's body:

*There'll soon be another woman, Anna. An ex-girlfriend in a bath of acid. Or a young jogger who never makes it home. That's just how things are. Women aren't safe.*

There'd been a clinical eeriness in Assumpta's delivery that had left Anna unsettled. The familiar warmth and spark had gone now, a world-weary cynicism taking up residence in its place. Was it any wonder, Anna thought. A man's violence had ended her only daughter's life, and no amount of well-intentioned op-eds or national hand-wringing would change the fact that Ger was destined to be just another tragic statistic.

Sergeant Rooney would pop in to see Anna at Juliette's most afternoons. Dan's trial was scheduled at the Central Criminal Court for early March. Rooney had confirmed he wouldn't get bail due to the gravity of the charges and the fact he was considered a flight risk. They had enough evidence to push things along relatively quickly, including samples of Ger's blood on his shovel and in Anna's car. Dan had admitted returning to Anna's house on the night he'd buried Ger, to pick up the clothes she'd been wearing earlier that evening, along with her phone and wallet. He'd thrown everything into a skip out the front of a derelict house, all evidence gone by the time Anna had awoken that Friday morning with the last hangover she'd ever have. The swatch of fabric Anna had found in Cassidy's shack during their weekend away had simply been similar in colour to the top Ger had been wearing in the pub, taken from something worn by one of the sex workers Cassidy had terrorised, a sick little relic for his trophy collection. At least the cops had Cassidy on their radar now. A hefty list of charges was being compiled. He'd been added to the sex offenders' register too.

And the white van Ger had encountered on her walk home? They'd never know who the driver was. It probably was just someone looking for directions, after all. But it didn't actually matter now anyway. Ger had been killed by someone known to her, not a stranger. Wasn't that often the way?

In the initial weeks after they'd arrested Daniel, there had been many sleepless nights when Anna would let herself quietly out of Juliette's house and walk for hours. She'd always have a long screwdriver squirrelled into her jacket pocket, primed for violence but refusing to be cowed, as she walked the empty streets. And on more than one occasion, she'd found herself miles from home, standing on the frigid ground of the abandoned hotel site, near the low blackthorn tree where Ger's body had been found. Hours would pass, the stars her only witness, Anna praying for some forgiveness amid the caustic guilt that constantly swirled around her insides these days. Anna had brought Ger's killer into their lives and she'd never be able to undo that. But Daniel Pell, alone, had wrought this terrible act. He, alone, had killed Ger and dumped her body like a sack of garbage. He, alone, had caused unnecessary months of untold anguish by not coming forward. But Anna was no fool. Whatever words or rationale she used, she understood the self-blame would always trail her, keenly clinging to her like a shadow until her dying day.

At the start of December, Anna took aside her boss at *Houghton, Hartery & Lynch* and handed in her four weeks' notice. It was time, she'd said. Better to leave before she became jaded and demotivated. As she'd walked out of the office that evening, she had attempted to quell her rising panic by telling herself she would figure out her next move in the new year. But as she'd made her way through the Christmas shoppers to the train, her brain was already running ahead of her.

She'd had enough of simply making rich people richer. From now on she would shift her focus to where she could truly help. There were so many people lacking financial literacy. And there were countless families struggling with huge debt, at risk of falling through the cracks. Money would be tight, but she had enough savings to last her six months and it was beyond time to get out of her comfort zone. On the packed commuter train home that evening, as her plans began to crystallise, Anna had felt a comforting presence. She'd turned her head to the darkness speeding by outside the carriage window, and just for a split second, amid the reflected commuters in their scarfs and dull overcoats, she imagined she saw Ger beaming a smile at her, an encouraging glint in those gypsy eyes.

So, in the dwindling days of December, there was a small but steady fire in Anna's belly, a strange bedfellow to counter the aching grief which ailed her heart. She was keen to start this new chapter. But there was something else she needed to do first. A promise to an old friend.

# Later

# THIRTY-EIGHT

THE WARM PACIFIC LAPS AT THE SHORELINE and plays over the ochre sand. Early evening sunlight warms the pastel hues of the parasols which stud the gently curving cove, where nut-brown children play waist-deep in the aqua shallows along the water's edge as parents watch on laxly from sun loungers. From somewhere further along the beach a faint pulsating rhythm drifts up. A small group of drummers sit in a circle, their eyes closed, expressions of easy contentment on their faces. An elderly local man who has stopped to watch them breaks into a shuffling dance on the sand. It's a little piece of paradise. Well, almost...

It took her three flights to get here, the taxi from the local airport only dropping her off a few hours ago. Her suitcase remains unpacked, just inside the door of the one-bedroom apartment she's rented. Simple and clean, it's a cute little place with a ceiling fan, just up the sandy path, a hammock out front overlooking the beach.

She folds down the corner of her novel and lets her gaze settle on the blurred line of the horizon. This wasn't the plan, and she knows only too well that the next few weeks of travel will be full of bittersweet moments. It was supposed to be the pair of them, kicking off their adventures here in Puerto Escondido. Anna knows she could have just stayed back in Ireland and spent the first dark and difficult days of the new year in Juliette's. But if the past few months had taught her anything, it was not to put things off. She takes a long sip of water from her bottle. There are plenty of days still, when she struggles to put one foot in front of the other. But she does it nonetheless, choosing to believe that Ger is watching from the wings. Anna will aim to live a life that's big enough for both of them now. And she'll take nothing for granted.

She rakes her fingers through the warm sand, feels the first insistent tug of jet lag trying to pull her down into slumber. It's time to head up to the apartment. She'll shower off her sunscreen, maybe say hi to her neighbours. She sits up and stretches out her legs along the towel and can't help but laugh at her pasty skin. God, she really is the whitest thing on the beach.

She stands and shakes the sand from her towel. One of the drummers has lit a campfire and it throws a warm glow on the faces of the circle. Anna smiles at the simple pleasure of it all, then turns for the path up to the apartment. She stops, hesitates, and looks down the beach again. The old man continues his shuffling dance on the edge of the drum circle. But now a mother and her young daughter have joined in, and a few other random people too, everyone loosely swaying, smiling as they move, some awkward, some effortless. Anna's feet take her steadily down towards the group, the rhythm louder here, tribal and compelling. But she stands off to the side at a respectable distance, one of life's observers. Ger would have been in her element here, in amongst it, having a go. And Anna feels the hot sting of tears now. Tears for Ger's irreplaceable energy, stolen from them all too soon. But also tears of the most profound gratitude, that Anna got to enter Ger's orbit in the first place. Perhaps it's the jet lag which causes Anna to drop her towel and bag to the sand by her bare feet. But it doesn't really matter. She steps forward into the circle of strangers. She smiles through her tears at the mother, at the old man, at the whole messy bunch of beautiful humanity. She closes her eyes, sees her friend, and lets the rhythm take over. She'll dance for them both now.

# Dear Reader...

Thank you for picking up my book. I really hope you enjoyed *The Stranger's Bed*.

If you'd like to be kept informed about new releases and special offers, simply zap the QR code and fill in your name and email address. No spam ever – and you can unsubscribe at any time.

# Author's Note

I must admit to taking one or two liberties with the geographical layout and features of Skerries village in North County Dublin. It's a place of which I'm very fond and I try to visit at least once a year. With that said, I'm hoping any locals reading this story haven't had a conniption at my omission of the train tracks which, in part, run parallel to the Balbriggan Road. It was a necessary evil to fit the story into the place (or vice versa), so don't send any angry missives my way please. There may also be some subtle nudges of street length, etc.,          but I'm sure you can forgive me those...

The spelling in this story is in UK-English as opposed to US-English. So 'kilometre' instead of 'kilometer'; 'neighbour' instead of 'neighbor'; 'grey' instead of 'gray', etc. For the Aussie Readers, I've dipped into my 20+ years of living in Sydney to aim for a good degree of realism with Dan's dialogue. But if you feel I've committed any sins I'm happy to be corrected! Both Irish and Australian slang have been used throughout.

A big shout-out to my early readers on this book, namely Sally H, Dara M and Kevin M. You're all amazeballs.

And once again, here's to you, Dear Reader, for taking a punt on this book in the first place.

Many thanks and stay well,

*Oliver Sands*

www.ingramcontent.com/pod-product-compliance
Lightning Source LLC
Chambersburg PA
CBHW020007140726
47904CB00018B/1994